Katie was stunned by the fierce possessiveness of Adrian's kiss.

It was as if he had been dancing around her ever since they had met, but had at last swooped in to claim her as his, finally and forever. And now that she knew something about him she was ready to let him in. She let herself flow into that possession, welcoming it, opening her mouth when his tongue slid along the seam of her lips.

She slid her hands from his chest around his leanly fleshed ribs and across his back. Beneath the soft cotton of his shirt she could feel the muscles she had admired that day in the pool, except that his mouth was distracting her. There was just too much sensation to revel in, tongue now lightly touching lips, now plunging deep, again playful. His hands moved from her upper arms across her back, and down the length of the muscles along each side of her spine to the small of her waist. They only paused there a moment before sliding over the curve of her rump to pull her hips forward into a more intimate contact with his.

She felt him against the length of her, thighs touching thighs, muscled abdomen touching belly, chest pressed to breasts, and all of him, including that part pressed to her groin, was hard and urgent.

How could he be so hard when she was turning to liquid?

Other books and Stories by Michele Stegman

Fortune's Foe

Fortune's Pride

Conquest of the Heart

"The Shrew That Tames"

"A Pirate's Tale"

"The Admirer"

"The Christmas Pony"

"A Book of Life and a Trick" in *How I Met My Husband*

"Samaurai Cat" in *Cats on the Keyboard*

Mr. Right's Baby

MICHELE STEGMAN

MYTHICAL PRESS ★ DAYTON, OHIO

Mr. Right's Baby

ISBN 978-0-9967976-2-7
Copyright © 2011 by Michele Stegman
Cover art © 2016 Jennette Marie Powell Heikes
Hat and gloves photo used under license via www.bigstockphoto.com
Other photos © 2016 Michele Stegman

This story is a work of fiction. Names, characters, places, and incidents are either products of the author's imagination or are used fictitiously. Any resemblance to actual events, locales, business establishments, media titles, or persons living or dead, is entirely coincidental.

Dedication

To the Erdmans, Dan, Marcia, Laura and Katie,
for many years of friendship.

One

HER DESK WAS STILL EMPTY. SURELY SHE WOULDN'T MISS today. Not after he had waited so long. With a smile, Adrian Wright stood by the door of the first grade classroom welcoming each student who entered, a hand on the head to ruffle the hair of the boys, bending to help pick up dropped lunches or hair barrettes, answering the inevitable question of, "Are you Mrs. Sandy's substitute?" at least twelve times. But still she did not come.

The clock was moving steadily toward eight and the room was fast filling up, but her desk was still empty—except for a well-chewed, fat, red pencil in the groove at the top. Her name, stuck onto the front of the desk at the beginning of the school year with sticker paper, was badly frayed from eight months of chairs and desks bumping, and stained from several dribbles of watercolor, but it was still legible. Carly Simmons.

The students were putting lunches in the coatroom, emptying book bags, putting homework papers on Mrs. Sandy's desk. They were talking and laughing freely, but were quiet and orderly. Mrs. Sandy had taught them well. About half of them had hair ranging from almost pure white to tow heads to light brown. The other half were dark-haired, dark-eyed Hispanics. Carly wasn't Hispanic, but he thought she would have dark hair. Like his.

The corridor was clearing as kids made a last minute dash for their classrooms. There were only three or four children left and they were older, third or fourth grade. Adrian grasped the doorknob to close the door. Maybe tomorrow, then. Maybe she would be here tomorrow.

A little girl suddenly came skidding around the corner of the hallway, long, dark braids flying, one of them already loose, the red ribbon dangling. She charged straight toward Mrs. Sandy's classroom doorway and straight into his heart. It was her

She was perfect. She was just as he had imagined her ever since he had learned of her existence six months ago. Her hair was, indeed, black like his. Black and shiny, and he wanted to touch it to see if it was as soft and silky as it looked. He held out a hand. He had patted the other kids on the head as they came in. But this time, his hand was shaking too badly so he let it drop. It wasn't just his hand that was shaking. He thought his legs might crumble beneath him if he weren't gripping the doorknob like an anchor in an emotional storm.

Carly caught herself with one hand on the doorframe and looked up at him, a big smile showing a perfect row of baby teeth she hadn't yet lost. "Are you Mrs. Sandy's substitute?" she asked.

Adrian tried to swallow the golf ball that had suddenly lodged in his throat. Unsuccessful, he merely nodded. Carly skipped on into the room, thumped her book bag onto the seat beside her desk, and started putting her books into her desk. Several girls gathered around her, one of them pointing out Carly's loosened braid. Carly pulled the elastic band from the end of her other braid and loosened it as well, leaving her hair in two, nearly waist length ponytails slightly waved from being held briefly in braids.

She was beautiful. He wanted to go right in there and scoop her up, and give her the seven years of hugs he had missed out on giving her. He wanted to feel her arms around his neck and hear her call him "Daddy."

But the little girl putting her homework paper on the teacher's desk had no idea he was her father. Maybe she didn't even know she had been adopted, given up without her father's knowledge or consent. All she knew of him was that while Mrs. Sandy was out having a baby, he was her substitute for the three weeks left of the school year. She didn't even know his name.

Adrian took just a moment to compose himself, gritting his teeth and taking a deep breath, before he had to go in there and treat her like any other child.

"First day jitters?" Mrs. Webb, the kindergarten teacher next door, was just reaching out to shut her door when she saw him. She smiled and shoved an unruly mop of blond curls off her forehead. "You'll do fine," she assured him. "I'll be right here if you need me. But Carly Simmons can help you out with classroom routine. She's a great kid."

"Carly." He could barely get the name out, but managed a smile "I'll remember. Thanks."

She nodded and closed her door, calling to an Edward to stop bouncing a ball.

When Adrian closed his own classroom door, he turned to find Carly standing there waiting for him. "Can you tie this for me?" she asked, pulling at the ribbon that still dangled from her ponytail. It had been tied over an elastic band that still held the ponytail in place.

To Adrian it was a wonderful gift she was giving him, the right to tie a bow in her hair. Adrian took the ribbon, the backs of his fingers touching her hair. She tilted her head to give him better access and he tried to keep his hands from shaking as he performed this small service for her.

"Thank you," she said, reaching up to touch the slightly

crooked bow before skipping to her seat.

"Thank you," he almost said before changing it quickly to, "You're welcome."

Adrian took up a piece of chalk, called the class to order and turned to write his name on the board. "This is my name," he told the class, "Mr. Wright."

The rest of the class simply nodded and sat waiting for him to continue, but he heard an audible gasp from Carly. Her eyes widened and her hand shot up.

"Yes?"

"Is that really who you are?" she asked. "Are you really Mr. Wright?"

Puzzled by her attitude, Adrian laughed and assured her that he really was Mr. Wright. Then he passed out a math worksheet Mrs. Sandy had left for him and started the day.

For Adrian, the day spent with his daughter was a joy almost too painful to accept. He knew he gave her more attention than he gave anybody else. But he couldn't help it. He watched her add teeth marks to her pencil as she worked. He watched her play kick ball at recess. He watched her line up and go down to the cafeteria clutching a pink Barbie lunch box.

At lunchtime, he looked at her school records. It was just as the detective who had found her told him. Mother's name: Kathryn. Father: Brent, deceased.

By two-thirty, he had had about as much joy as he could hold for one day. His daughter seemed healthy, happy, and well-adjusted. She was outgoing and friendly, and very intelligent. He still wanted to know about her home life. What kind of mother was Kathryn Simmons? Loving? Gentle? Stern? Strict?

And somehow, he wanted to be a part of Carly's life. Unlike the woman who had given birth to her, there was no way he could just walk away from her.

As he led the class out to the buses, he allowed himself to pat her on the head, small compensation for all the good night kisses and bedtime stories he had been denied. She looked up at him. "My mom is supposed to pick me up. I hope she comes."

An alarm went off in Adrian's heart. Was her mother unreliable? Irresponsible? "Does she usually pick you up?" he asked.

Carly nodded, anxiously scanning the cars lined up in front of the school next to a row of yellow buses. "There she is! She came!" A wide smile of relief played over her face as she pointed to a sporty red car just rolling to a halt at the end of the line.

Adrian's brows crunched together at the sight of that car. He had envisioned a Toyota mini van or a Ford Escort. What was the mother of his child doing jaunting around in a flashy sports car? A flashy *red* sports car.

"Come on! You've got to meet her!" Carly was tugging at his hand, urging him toward the car. And her mother.

He definitely wanted to meet this woman.

"Just a minute, Carly. I have bus duty." He squeezed her hand holding her there, savoring the tang of joy that surged through his heart as her trusting fingers clasped his.

One boy jostled another getting on the bus and Adrian pulled him aside, holding his shoulder, making him wait until last. The boy fidgeted, Carly kept jumping up and down, but Adrian was the most impatient of all. At last the bus was loaded, the boy leapt up the steps, and Adrian let Carly tow him along toward that red car.

The door swung open even before Carly reached it, letting out a blast of rock music along with a stream of cold air. She tossed her book bag and lunch box behind the seat and bounced in. "Mom! I found him! I found Mr. Right. Now you can get married!"

Adrian's brows arched. Looking for Mr. Right, huh? So she was man hunting. Adrian bent down to get his first look at Kathryn Simmons. By this time he was expecting a barracuda with long red nails impatiently tapping the steering wheel.

She was not what he expected. She was worse. A dirty white gym shoe with a toe poking out sat on the brake. The leg was shapely enough to give Adrian's loins a lurch, except that there was some unidentifiable smear of sludge on the calf and a half-healed scrape on the knee. A slash of rusty brown cut across both thighs and a smudge of black grease went from thigh to a pair of cut off jeans that looked like they had been run over by a herd of cattle. There was a spate of bare midriff topped by an unwieldy pair of what Adrian could only think of as boobs, large and round and barely held in check by a once white shirt tied across the ribs. A strand of shoulder length blond hair streaked by sun and grime fell from a lopsided ponytail only tentatively held in place by a yellow elastic band. Her face, with its pug nose, softly rounded pink mouth, and wide blue eyes would have been more attractive without dirty brown and black streaks.

Adrian gritted his teeth and managed to be polite. "Hello, Mrs. Simmons. I'm Adrian Wright, Mrs. Sandy's substitute for the rest of the year."

Kathryn Simmons jabbed at the radio, cutting off the din, curling her fingers into fists and crossing her arms to hide broken nails lined with black. At that maneuver, her boobs threatened to escape and she shifted, risking a quick tug to her shirt before hiding her hands again.

"See, Mom? Mr. Right! I found him!" Carly was on her knees on the seat.

"Oh! Oh no, Honey! I didn't mean..." Mrs. Simmons's blush didn't stop at her face. It traveled down her throat right down to the curve of those awesome boobs. She looked at Adrian, horrified. "I'm sorry. She doesn't understand. I..." She swallowed hard and nodded her head. "Nice meeting you, Mr. Wright." She put the car into gear and Adrian took the hint to move back.

Adrian watched the car fade into the traffic. Well, not fade. Not that car. A helpless trepidation stole over him and he wondered about the wisdom of leaving his daughter in the care of Mrs. Kathryn Simmons.

"Mom, are you going to marry Mr. Wright?"

Katie could still feel the hot flush that suffused her skin and wished she could have turned red enough to have blended into the red leather seat and disappeared. "I don't think so, Sweetie."

Carly's face wrinkled into a petulant frown. "But you said when you met Mr. Right, you'd marry him and I'd have a daddy again."

"That's just an expression, Honey. It means I'll get married when I meet the right person."

"Oh." Carly slumped down in her seat. A second later she looked up hopefully. "But Mr. Wright is really nice, Mom. The whole class thinks so."

"I'm sure he is," Katie said, not at all sure it was true. Mr. Wright seemed a little foreboding to her, scowling at her the way he had. In other circumstances she would have called a man who looked like that dangerous. Dangerously attractive. It made her nipples taut just thinking about him. A reaction she hadn't had since... She slowed, both the car and her thinking, to turn into their street.

Anybody who'd scowl at me like that can't possibly be the real Mr. Right, Katie thought, then took a quick inventory of the way she looked. She wasn't anything to smile at right now. The time had just gotten away from her and she had had to leave the gutters half cleaned to get to school on time. She knew how Carly would panic if she were even a few minutes late.

Katie pulled into the driveway, eased into the garage and shut off the engine.

Carly pulled out her lunch box and book bag. "Can I get in the pool?"

"Sure. Just wait until I'm out there. You know the rule."

Carly nodded and bounced into the house. Katie put her head down on the steering wheel. *I will never, ever be able to face that man again*, she thought.

Sighing, Katie lifted her head and leaned back in the seat. The gutters were calling. Katie was calling. The bread she had left rising was calling. She went into the house and washed her hands.

Carly bounced into the kitchen in her new yellow swim suit and watched while Katie punched down the bread dough and put it into the pans for the second rising. "Can I get in the pool now, Mom?"

"In just a minute, Sweetie. I have to get the ladder from the side of the house. As soon as I'm in the back, you can get in."

Carly went out to the back yard and Katie went to get the ladder.

The ladder was propped against the side of the house. Katie reached for it, glad she didn't have a two story house. She couldn't have handled a ladder that long. This one was awkward enough. There had been a downpour that morning—a downpour that had overflowed the gutters letting her know they needed cleaning out. But the ground was still soft from the rain and the ladder was stuck. Katie tugged again and tried to jiggle it loose. She felt it give. Suddenly there were arms around her and she didn't have to turn around to know who they belonged to.

"Why don't you let me help you with that?" The voice of her neighbor was soft and silky in her ear. One of his hands covered one of hers on the ladder. The other slid around her waist, making the most of the bare skin at her midriff.

Katie pulled his hand off her waist as she would have pulled off a leech. "Thanks, Mitch. I think I can handle it."

"But there's no need to now that I'm here." His free hand grasped the other side of the ladder, trapping her between two muscular arms and one knucklehead.

Pulling her hand free and drawing her arms up across her chest, Katie managed to turn in the narrow space between Mitch and the ladder. She thought if she confronted him face-to-face, he would back off. She was wrong.

He leaned into her, pressing her back against the ladder. His blond hair curled enticingly over a broad brow and cool blue eyes. He was handsome. And he knew it. He gave her a lopsided grin that she supposed was meant to be boyishly winning. If only his brain was as strong as his arms, he would be quite a catch.

"How about going to the Spurs game with me Friday night?"

"I don't think so, Mitch." She placed her hands against his chest and pushed. It was rock hard and may as well have actually been made of stone for all the good her efforts did her.

"You really are quite a woman, Katie," Mitch said. She noticed that his gaze was not on her face but on her breasts which were pressed up between them.

"Thank you, Mitch, but I really need to get to work now."

He sighed and released her. Nudging her aside he easily picked up the ladder with one hand. "Where do you want this thing?"

Adrian closed and locked the classroom door and headed out into the bright May sunshine. He knew her address. He had already driven by her house twice. There had been no one outside either time, but he would drive by again. It wasn't far and he just might see her playing in the yard, maybe riding a bike.

He drove down her street slowly. The garage door was open and he could see the red sports car inside. No one was out front. But he nearly hit the breaks when the east side of the house came into view. The buxom Mrs. Simmons was leaning back against a ladder flirting outrageously with some tall, muscle-bound Nordic type. Her hands were on his chest and a sheet of paper wouldn't have fit between them.

He had tried to give her credit. He had convinced himself that she had been embarrassed by Carly's earlier remarks about looking for Mr. Right. But it looked like he'd been right the first time. She really was man hunting. It made him wonder just what went on in that house. What was his daughter being exposed to?

If he went any slower he would have to stop and that would attract too much attention. So he gritted his teeth, gripped the wheel and kept going. But he caught a last glimpse of Mr. Muscle carrying the ladder for her as she followed along, her fanny jiggling just right in her tight denim shorts.

Two

As soon as Adrian pulled into the parking lot of the H.E.B. grocery he spotted a familiar fanny. It was the same compact little backside that had intruded into his thoughts more often than he cared to admit during the last two days. By the time Adrian had parked, Mrs. Simmons was bent over, packing cases of beer into the trunk of her sports car.

"Can I give you a hand?"

"Oh!" Mrs. Simmons straightened with a start. "Mr. Wright! You scared me."

"Sorry," Adrian apologized. He quickly took in the sight of her trim figure. She still had four cases of beer and four bottles of wine in her cart, but she didn't look like she actually drank much of it. Just a small waist and a belly that curved with femininity, not beer. She "cleaned up good," too. Her hair, even lighter blond now that it was clean, curved over her collar bone as if inviting his hand to brush it back behind her shoulders. She wore a dash of makeup. The sweat and black streaks were gone, revealing a smooth, peaches-and-cream complexion that went all the way down to where her blush had gone two days ago. Today, a more conservative top covered a bit more of her, but nothing could conceal the rich swell of what lay beneath that powder blue cotton.

"May I?" he asked, reaching for one of the cases.

"Thank you." She moved aside to let him pile the cases in the trunk.

The last thing to go in was a carton of cigarettes. Adrian couldn't help but frown when he tossed those in. Didn't she know what secondary smoke did to young lungs?

"Carly talks about you a lot, Mr. Wright. She's really enjoying your class."

Mrs. Simmons's voice was smooth and sweet as honey. It seemed to reach right inside him and twitch every one of his organs, his heart, his stomach, his...

"Adrian," he said, almost not getting the word out. Her voice seemed to have affected his lungs as well.

"What?" she asked, surprised at his non sequitur.

"My first name is Adrian." Teachers might not ordinarily encourage students' parents to call them by their given names, but Adrian wanted to get to know this woman. Because of Carly, of course.

"Oh. Mine's Katie." Giving a quick, nervous laugh, she stuck out her hand. "Nice to meet you, now that I'm not looking quite so disreputable as the first time."

Adrian gave his eyes the treat of looking her over a second time. "No," he said, "not disreputable at all." It was good to know she realized just how bad an impression she had given him when he had first met her. He took her hand. It was not as soft as he had expected. It was firm and strong. He didn't want to let go, but he did. Physically, anyway. His mind tended to hold on to the feel of her fingers, even after he tucked his own into his back pocket.

"Carly's a great kid," Adrian said. "My first day, the kindergarten teacher told me Carly could help me out if I had any problems."

Katie's eyes softened and she chuckled softly. "She's always wanted to help out. Even when she was more trouble than help."

"She's certainly been no trouble at school. I couldn't ask for a better dau...student." Adrian suddenly began looking everywhere but into her eyes. "Where is Carly?" he asked, letting out a little laugh. Not home alone while her mother is out buying beer and cigarettes, he hoped.

"At Angela Kisor's."

"Angela Kisor?" he questioned, knowing she expected the name to mean something to him. "Oh! Yes! Little red- haired girl. Freckles on top of freckles. Sits right behind Carly."

"That's the one."

He shrugged apologetically. "I don't know all the kids' names yet."

"You've only been there three days. Give yourself time." She touched him briefly on the arm. He was sure it was just a sympathetic touch to reinforce her words, but she managed to put a tangle in his guts just the same.

"Angela and Carly are best friends and the Kisors live just two doors away, which makes it very convenient. For both of us."

"I guess so. It must be difficult being a single parent."

"How did you know I was a single parent?"

"I...I...uh...I had to record some information on the school records. I just noticed it."

"I see."

There went that blush again, her face, her throat, right on down beneath that blue blouse. He'd put his foot into it enough for one day. Best to make an exit while he could still do it somewhat gracefully.

She must have been thinking the same thing for they both spoke at once.

"I'd better get the groceries I came for and get home."

"I'd better get this beer home while it's still cold."

They shifted uneasily, then again spoke at once.

"Well, good-bye, Mr. Wr...Adrian."

"See you later, Mrs. Sim...Katie."

He grinned and waved and hurried into the store.

She turned and got into her car.

Substitutes don't record things into the school records, she thought. *He looked it up on purpose. He wanted to know if I was attached.* She smiled to herself, pleased, yet frustrated—there weren't any records she could look at to see if *he* was attached. She'd have to find out some other way.

A horn beeped and she jumped. A car was trying to pull into the place next to her. She had been so bemused she hadn't realized she was sitting there with the car door open.

Hastily she shut the door and jammed the key into the ignition, embarrassed by the line her thoughts had taken. It wasn't until she was pulling into her street that she realized what Adrian Wright had helped load into her car. Four cases of beer, wine, and cigarettes. Why couldn't she have mentioned that it was all for her neighbor? Even though Mrs. Winsted was in a wheelchair her family still had their reunion at her house every year. She was just helping Mrs. Winsted out.

She was also going to do the baking for Mrs. Winsted's party— bread and buns for sandwiches and barbeque, a rum cake, carrot cake, and two apple pies. Her reputation was getting around. She had gotten a call that morning from a complete stranger who had heard about her baking skills from a friend and wanted her to do the desserts for an elaborate garden party.

Next week she was going to have business cards printed, and soon, very soon, she promised herself, she was going to open her own small bakery.

Not that she needed the money. Brent had been a real insurance freak and had left her and Carly very well taken care of. But running a bakery had always been a dream of hers. That and having a house full of kids. That last thought always brought a lump of sadness to her throat. No need to start thinking of that again, she chided herself.

Mrs. Winsted had wheeled herself out to the driveway to meet Katie and now her neighbor grinned, waving a cigarette laden hand.

"You're a doll to pick up all this stuff for me," Mrs. Winsted said, rasping and wheezing. "Just put it in the fridge in the garage."

Katie started hauling cases. "I'm going to bake the bread and buns tomorrow," she said, "and make the rum cake Friday."

"Be sure to put plenty of rum in it."

Katie grinned. "No problem. I have a secret method for making sure even the middle of the cake is rum soaked. Your family is going to love it."

By Friday afternoon, Katie had everything done that Mrs. Winsted had ordered for her party. Miriam Kisor, Angela's mom, was watching both Carly and Angela out in the pool. All Katie needed to do was finish soaking the cake with the rum sauce and she could deliver everything to Mrs. Winsted. The cake had already soaked up a lot. She just had to add the final touch via her secret method.

She took out a clean hypodermic syringe to fill with rum and inject the cake. There wasn't much left in the sauce pan and she had to tilt it to get to the rum sauce. That's when the doorbell rang. At the same time, Angela cannon-balled into the pool shrieking with laughter, and the needle slipped. Rum sauce sloshed all over Katie's halter top, trickling down between her breasts, and she just managed to catch the pan between her thighs against the cabinet.

Hastily, she wiped her hands and top with a dish towel and went to answer the door. She shoved a couple of Carly's toys out of the way but there wasn't much she could do about the mess in the living room. Not with half the furniture out getting reupholstered, the curtains in the washer, and everything off the walls for the painter to start painting tomorrow. Anyone coming into this house for the first time today would not get a good impression of the place.

By Friday afternoon, as Adrian pushed the last kid onto a bus, he was more exhausted than he had ever been on any nine-to-five job he had ever had. It was a joyful exhaustion, but he wondered how teachers did it week after week, year after year.

He had watched Carly's anxious face turn to relief when they came outside to see Katie's red sports car pulled up to the curb with the other cars. Not once had Katie been late picking up Carly. Why then was Carly so anxious? It was a worry that nagged at him every day when he saw the tension start growing in Carly just before dismissal.

He walked back into the building and into the classroom to get the pile of papers he had to grade. He was just shoving them into his briefcase when he saw it. Carly's Little Stripey Tiger.

The stuffed animal was lying in Adrian's chair looking woefully up at him, probably missing Carly as much as she would miss it tonight. Carly had put the tiger on his desk after the show-and-tell session and another child must have knocked it off when they added their display. By the time show-and-tell was over, Carly's dismissal tension was beginning to build and the tiger, out of sight behind the desk, had been left behind.

Adrian couldn't resist cuddling the tiger under his chin, smelling it, feeling Carly holding the animal every night. Her father had given it to her, she'd said, just before he left on a trip, so it could hug her while he was gone. Now he was gone forever. But she still had Little Stripey Tiger.

Adrian wondered if she would cry herself to sleep without it tonight. Maybe the whole weekend. Not if he could help it. He closed up the room, went out to his car, put the tiger in the passenger seat, and headed for Carly's house.

He had been looking for an excuse to stop at Carly's home, to see inside, to get closer to her. This was perfect. She might even see him coming with her tiger and run to give him a hug. It made him feel all warm and fuzzy inside just thinking of Carly's arms around his neck. Katie would be there, too, smiling indulgently at them, gratitude glowing in her cornflower blue eyes.

Thinking of Katie the way he had last seen her made him feel entirely different. Warm, maybe, but definitely not fuzzy.

Adrian pulled into the driveway, tucked the tiger under one arm and went to the door. When it opened, all his fantasies dissolved in the reek of rum that oozed out to meet him. Katie stood there in the doorway, her rose pink mouth formed into a round O of surprise, her green halter top soaked and clinging to her lush curves.

Even with the alcoholic fumes she looked good enough to make Adrian's heart lurch, but he clamped down on any vestiges of tenderness still lingering from his fantasy of being met at the door by Carly and a fond mother. Instead, he looked beyond her into the room, telling himself that he only wanted to see what kind of home Carly lived in.

It couldn't have been worse. There was no touch of the comfortable hominess he had hoped for for his daughter. No pictures of a close family on the walls, no mementos of happy days on the mantle, not even much furniture.

"Adrian! I...come in."

His gaze came back to the woman in front of him, but he couldn't smile. He held out the tiger.

"Little Stripey Tiger! How...?" She took the stuffed animal and absently rubbed its head.

"Carly brought it for show-and-tell and left it at school. It seemed to mean a lot to her. I thought I'd bring it by." His voice sounded gruff, even to him. He cleared his throat.

"I appreciate it. Carly's father gave it to her and she sleeps with it every night."

"She told us in show-and-tell." Katie didn't seem drunk, he thought. Her words weren't slurred. Maybe she was just getting started.

"I see." She looked down at the tiger and seemed lost in thought for a moment.

"Where is Carly?" he asked.

She snapped back to the present. "Out in the pool. I was just working in the kitchen." She gestured vaguely toward the back of the house.

Fear gripped Adrian's heart. Carly was out in the pool and her mother was in the kitchen? He clenched his teeth, as well as his fists, to keep from reaching out, shaking her and yelling at her for her inattentive care. Instead he gritted out, "I'd better go. You'll be wanting to check on her."

"No, I..." She stopped, a look of concern crossing her face. "Are you all right?"

"Am I... Yes. Yes, I'm fine. Good-bye, Mrs. Simmons." Abruptly, he turned and hurried down the walk to his car.

Mrs. Simmons? Katie blinked in surprise. "I thought we were on a first name basis," she muttered, watching him slam his car door and grip the wheel like he wanted to crunch it into croutons. What was bothering the once again scowling Mr. Wright, she wondered, scowling a bit herself.

She put Little Stripey Tiger down on the one remaining living room chair and returned to the kitchen and her rum cake.

Rum. She knew she reeked of it. Had the haughty Mr. Wright gotten the impression that she was some kind of rummy?

She replayed their conversation in her head. Everything had been going along fine until he had asked about Carly. What had she said that was so bad? Then it dawned on her. She hadn't mentioned that Miriam and Angela were in the pool with Carly. He thought she had left Carly unsupervised in the pool. What business was it of his anyway? She didn't know whether to be mad that he thought she could be so irresponsible or glad to know Carly had such a concerned teacher.

Anger won out.

She filled the syringe with rum and jabbed it into the cake wishing it were Mr. Wright's backside instead. But that made her think of what nice tight buns he had. The fact that he could be so disconcerting that way, in spite of his scowls, made her even madder.

Miriam came into the kitchen, shooing the two girls ahead of her. Katie almost snapped at Carly before she realized that it wasn't her daughter she was mad at, and Carly was not dripping water all over as usual. Her suit was still wet, but not enough to matter.

"Mmm. Looks wonderful," Miriam said. "I'll have to order one of those the next time I have a party."

"I'll be glad to do it for you, and no charge," Katie answered. "After all the babysitting you do for me, I owe you."

"I'll take you up on that. Come on Angie. We have to go get dressed. Daddy's taking us out to dinner."

Angie gave a gap-toothed grin. "Can we go to Alamo Cafe?"

Miriam laughed. "Do you think that's the only restaurant in town?"

"No, but it's my favorite."

Miriam laughed again and waving good-bye shooed her

daughter out the door ahead of her.

Carly climbed up on a stool, sat on her towel, and leaned on the counter to watch Katie finish the cake.

"I like that cake but not when you put that stuff in it."

"The rum?"

"Yeah." She watched as Katie finished soaking the cake and began to clean up. "Why do grown ups like that stuff?"

Katie smiled at her daughter. "I don't know, but they do."

"They must. You sure make a lot of those cakes."

"I sell a lot of these cakes," Katie said proudly.

"Will you sell them in your bakery?"

"I sure hope so." She covered the cake and turned on the dishwasher. "Let's go get those tangles out of your hair."

As they went through the living room, Katie picked up Little Stripey Tiger and handed him to Carly. "Mr. Wright was here. You left Little Stripey Tiger at school and he brought him home to you."

"Mr. Wright was here? Why didn't you tell me? I wanted to see him. He's so nice. I like Mr. Wright."

Katie looked down into her daughter's disappointed face. "Mr. Wright couldn't stay, Honey. He didn't even come in." Well, that was certainly true. He had stormed down the walk like no enticement in the world could have lured him inside. Not that she wanted to entice or lure him, she reminded herself.

"Oh. Okay." Dragging Little Stripey Tiger by one paw, Carly headed down the hall to the bathroom. Katie followed.

After her bath and hair wash, Carly talked about Mr. Wright. He was bringing pizza for the class on Monday because everyone had passed the spelling test. He played monster on the playground, chasing everyone around. He told long stories after lunch every day. He read Katie's favorite book out loud to the class. He brought in a real Indian beaded vest for show-and-tell. There seemed to be no end to the wonders of Mr. Wright.

"Doesn't Mr. Wright ever frown or get mad?" Katie asked, thinking that this paragon of a teacher must surely have his off moments. She certainly saw enough of his scowls.

"No, Mom. He laughs all the time. Even more than Mrs. Sandy." Carly looked thoughtful for a moment. "Well, there was one time he got a little mad. When the third grade boys were picking on Josh Miller again. Mr. Wright made them stop."

"Well, good for Mr. Wright!" Mr. Wright seemed like two different people, Katie thought. Scowls for her. Smiles for his class.

Katie finished drying Carly's hair and worked it into one long braid down her back. "Now why don't you do your homework while I fix us some supper?"

"I don't have any. Mr. Wright says he never gives homework on Fridays."

"In that case, you can help me fix supper."

Carly jumped up and ran to her bookbag. "But I do have some papers for you." She pulled out a sheaf of papers and handed them to Katie.

There were some tests and graded homework papers, and a letter to parents from Mr. Wright introducing himself and asking for volunteers to help with a class play. Katie looked at the letter thoughtfully. Mr. Wright didn't say much about himself. Just a lot of what she already knew. But the idea of helping with a class play was interesting. It would give her a chance to see first hand just how he handled the kids without actually demanding to sit in on his class.

She looked at the list of what was needed. She could make costumes. She filled out the bottom of the sheet and gave it back to Carly.

"Are you going to help with our play?" Carly's eyes glistened eagerly.

"Sure, if Mr. Wright needs me. I'll help make the costumes."

"That's great, Mommy. You're the best sew-er in the world."

Katie smiled. "Thank you very much. Now let's go fix that spaghetti."

Chapter Three

ADRIAN TRIED TO RELAX THE STRANGLEHOLD HE HAD ON the steering wheel. He was calling his lawyer. He wanted his daughter away from that woman. Carly might be upset for a while, but she would be better off in a home where she would be looked after. It would still be a one parent home, but at least he didn't get sloshed every Friday night and go chasing after women.

That rum-sodden, man-hunting, smoker didn't deserve a child like Carly. Carly deserved better. And he could give it to her. He would give it to her. She would be his, know who he was, know he had not given her away.

Monday morning. First thing. Calling his lawyer.

He slammed into his parking spot at the apartment complex where he had made his temporary home, yanked the emergency brake on, and headed down the live oak-shaded walk to his apartment.

"I never saw you scowl like that on a Friday before. School teaching must be getting to you."

"Jace!" Adrian dropped his briefcase and caught his brother up into a crushing bear hug, pounding him on the back nearly as much as he was getting pounded.

Still gripping Jace's shoulder, Adrian stepped back to arm's length to get a good look at his brother. "You're thinner. Downright skinny."

"Blame New Guinea."

"Got it all mapped?"

Jace laughed. "Sure. The whole country."

"Right." Adrian picked up his briefcase and unlocked the door. "Come on in. It ain't much, but it's home."

Jace looked around at the single chair, the portable TV propped on the same table as a lamp, and a pile of first grade school books. He whistled, shaking his head.

"Told you it wasn't much."

"The question is, what are you doing here?"

Adrian dropped his keys and case on the kitchen counter and went around to pull a couple of soft drinks out of the fridge. Handing one to Jace, he popped his open and took a long drink before he asked, "How long were you gone? Two, three months? Three. That's why you haven't heard."

"Heard what?"

Adrian motioned with his pop can toward the living room.

Jace sat on the floor and leaned against the wall, shaking his head at Adrian's offer of the chair. "I'm used to the floor after three months of nothing but floor to sit on."

Adrian shrugged and sat down, leaning forward to prop his elbows on his knees, the pop dangling from one hand. "I found her."

"Who?"

"My daughter."

Jace nearly choked on his pop, spluttered, and looked up at Adrian in shock. "Daughter? I didn't know you had a daughter."

"I didn't either until just a few weeks ago."

Jace took another drink, cocking a questioning brow in encouragement for his brother to continue.

"Remember Allison?"

Jace's brow knotted up trying to remember, but he shook his head.

"Eight years ago, blond..."

"Ditsy, more than amply endowed?" Jace's eyes lit, remembering. "Told you she was trouble."

"You were right. She wanted to get married. I didn't. Hell, I wasn't even out of college yet."

"It wasn't your degree she had her eye on," Jace said, "or even you. It was your money. Go on."

"I guess I was less than tactful about getting free of her. She was furious."

"And pregnant?"

Adrian nodded. "But I didn't know it then."

"I'm surprised she didn't use her pregnancy to trap you. I know what a sucker you are for kids."

"So did she. She asked me what I would do if she were pregnant. I told her I'd take full responsibility for the child, but that I still didn't want to marry her."

Jace winced. "Ouch."

"Yeah. She swore she wasn't pregnant, but she was. She had the baby and gave it up for adoption, knowing it would kill me to know I had a kid out there somewhere beyond my reach. But she was saving the news for when it would hurt the hardest. She said she planned to wait until she heard I was getting married and tell me on my wedding day."

Jace set his can down. "What made her change her mind?"

"She's dying." Adrian looked down at his hands folded around the pop can. "Cancer. She called me from the hospital. Asked me to come. She looked... Well, you know what chemo does. She wanted to set things right before she died. She even signed a paper saying that the 'unknown' on her child's birth certificate is me."

"You shouldn't have any trouble getting custody."

"None at all. Especially not with our background."

Jace gave him a puzzled look.

"One quarter Commanche. No court in the country would keep an Indian child away from her Indian father, especially since I never gave up my rights."

"Which brings me back to my original question," Jace said. "What are you doing here teaching school instead of back in Austin running the company?"

"I couldn't just let the courts step in and yank Carly out of a home where she had been living all her life, away from the only parents she had ever known. Do you realize what that would do to a kid? I decided to check out her home, her parents, before I made any other move. That's when I found out that her teacher was going to be out the rest of the year and they needed a substitute." Adrian shrugged, smiling. "I took the substitute job so I could observe Carly close-hand. I thought that if she was in a good situation I wouldn't disturb it. I'd just insist on visitation rights. Maybe someday, when she was older, I'd tell her the whole story."

"Carly? That's her name?" Jace asked.

"Yeah." The harsh lines of Adrian's face melted into a soft smile. "Sweetest kid I ever met. Smiles all the time. Tons of friends. And she's smart. Straight A's."

"You sure she's yours?"

Adrian laughed, but he knew his brother's question was also a serious one. "Her heritage shows. She has black hair and brown eyes and beautiful tan skin." He held up a hand. "I'll still go ahead with a genetic test before I take custody, but I know she's mine."

Jace looked surprised. "You're going to take custody?"

"Hell, yes, I'm taking custody," Adrian snarled.

"Carly smiles all the time, has tons of friends, straight A's. She sounds happy and well adjusted to me. What's the problem?"

Growling, Adrian stood up and started pacing the short length of the living room. "That...that mother of hers, that's what."

Jace leaned forward, a concerned look filling his eyes.

"She's a lush, she smokes, she leaves Carly alone in the pool, and..." Adrian thought of Katie leading the way for her neighbor to carry her ladder for her, "she twitches that cute little ass of hers at every man who passes by."

"Has she twitched it at you?" Jace asked, grinning.

Adrian glared at his brother and turned back to his pacing.

"What about Carly's father?"

Adrian snapped around to face Jace, jabbing a thumb into his chest. "I'm her father, dammit!" He started to pace again, stopped, then turned to face his brother. "Oh, you mean her adoptive father. He was killed in a car accident three years ago."

Jace folded his hands behind his head and leaned back against the wall. "Seems to me something's missing."

Adrian propped his hands on his hips and waited for Jace to continue.

"If Carly is as great as you say, her mother couldn't possibly be as bad as you're painting her. There has to be something positive there that you're not seeing."

"So, what am I supposed to do? Just walk away and leave my daughter?" Adrian challenged.

"I'm not suggesting that," Jace said. "But I would give it a little more time. Observe the situation a little longer. Get to know Carly's mother. Maybe you can work something out."

Adrian heaved a huge sigh. "Maybe you're right." His shoulders dropped and he rolled his head back and forth to work some of the tension out. "I have two more weeks until the end of the school year. I'll give it 'til then."

Jace nodded approvingly and stood up checking his watch. "I've got to get back to Austin. Mama made me promise to show up for supper and she's making my favorite—a batch of tamales—to make sure I do. How about coming home for the weekend?" He glanced around with a wry grin. "Nothing much here to keep you."

"Mama's homemade tamales, huh? I think I will."

"By the way, have you told Mom and Dad they're grandparents?"

"Not yet. I wanted to see Carly. Make sure she's mine, first."

Jace nodded. "Good idea. Well, get your stuff. You can fly back with me."

Adrian looked askance at his brother. "In that antique of yours?"

"Best little plane ever made. I'll bring you back bright and early Monday morning."

Adrian groaned. "Double jeopardy." But he grinned and went to pack. He returned shortly with his overnight bag in hand. "Okay, Jace, I'm ready."

Jace held up a warning finger. "That's Uncle Jace, if you please."

By Monday morning Adrian felt like he had been away from his daughter for a month instead of just two days. He was so anxious to see her he almost scooped her up and hugged her when she came in. He wanted to ask about her weekend, what she had done, who she had played with, what she had played. Did she play "house" or play with Barbie dolls, or pretend she was a dolphin when she was in the pool? He had no idea. And he wanted to know. Wanted to know all about her.

When she came up to his desk to return the form about the class play, her fingers brushed his, and he felt like he had been given a tantalizing gift. He watched her go back to her desk to unpack the rest of her book bag before he opened the note.

Katie Simmons had volunteered to make the costumes for the play and to bring cookies for the performance the last day of school. Adrian grinned. Perfect, he thought. The lovely Mrs. Simmons would be spending a lot of time at school in the next two weeks. He would have a lot of time to get to know her. Might as well start tomorrow. He scribbled a note asking her to come in at the end of school tomorrow so they could discuss costumes.

The next morning Carly brought her mother's answer. She would be there after school. Adrian wasn't sure who was the most anxious for Mrs. Simmons to show up, him or Carly, and he wondered again just why Carly was so worried about whether or not her mother would show up.

But she did show up. She was waiting by the door as the kids filed out to the bus, following the kindergarten class and Mrs. Webb who had bus duty this week. Carly flew to her mother as soon as she saw her. Mrs. Simmons bent down to catch her. Carly jumped into her arms, hugging her and winding her legs around her waist to cling tightly.

Laughing, Katie hugged Carly right back then peeled her daughter off and set her down. "One of these days," she said to Carly, "you're going to be too big to do that."

Adrian watched Katie straighten her yellow scoop-necked top, that seemed to make her skin and hair glow, then smooth a hand over her matching skirt.

His palm itched to smooth it for her, to run it over that enticingly rounded hip. He forced himself to turn away, to busy himself with getting out the script for the play, to stop thinking about hips and boobs and thighs and slim legs, and feet in barely-nothing sandals.

"Here's the script." Adrian handed the four page script to Katie, careful not to let his fingers brush hers.

"I'm the Fairy Queen!" Carly was practically jumping up and down.

"The Fairy Queen! How wonderful!" Katie's hand ran caressingly over Carly's head and down one cheek. Then she looked questioningly at Adrian as if to ask if he had given Carly a special part because her mom was helping with the costumes.

Adrian shrugged. "The class wrote the play and everyone got to be whatever they wanted to be. There's also a Fairy Princess, two real princesses, a real queen, two famous singers and two movie stars. For the boys there are three dragons, four ninjas, and a police detective. They all have about the same amount to say."

"So, everyone feels they are the star of the show," Katie finished.

"Something like that. I always got stuck playing a tree, myself."

Katie laughed. "I was always one of about a dozen angels in the Christmas pageant."

He watched as she glanced through the script. Her nails were clean today. And so was the rest of her. He could smell the freshness of her from where he stood three feet away. As if she had just had a shower.

"I don't think the costumes will be much of a challenge," she said. "Godzilla was pretty popular last Halloween. I imagine there are still a few of those costumes around if you send home a note to parents asking for them. Fairy wings are easy to make with coat hangers and nylon. Crowns are easy to make."

"You certainly make it sound easy. What about material? Will you need some money to buy some?"

She shook her head. "Carly was a fairy for Halloween. I still have some nylon left over. I'll use that for the wings and fairy skirts. I have plenty of elastic and glitter."

"And we have my box of dress-ups," Carly said. "Leslie can

wear that sparkly dress to be the queen."

"You're right! That would work perfectly."

Carly beamed. "Can I go play on the playground?"

Katie glanced out the window. The playground was in full view. "Sure. We're almost done, I think."

Carly grabbed her book bag and lunch box, and sprinted out the door.

Adrian invited Katie to sit down and they discussed the other costumes. Katie noticed that Adrian glanced out the window to check on Carly more often than she did.

"I guess that's about it, then." Katie started to get up.

"There is one more thing I'd like to discuss, Mrs. Simmons... Katie."

"I was wondering if we were still on a first name basis. The last time I saw you, we didn't seem to be."

Adrian squirmed in his seat. If he wanted to get closer to her—and to Carly—he had to take it easy and not let his anger show, even if she did turn out to be an irresponsible lush. "I'm sorry about that. I...there was something..."

"Carly wasn't in the pool alone. Angela Kisor was with her. And Angela's mother. I would never leave Carly alone in the pool, and she knows not to even go close to it unless an adult is out there with her."

Adrian never knew he was capable of blushing, but he felt like he was doing just that right now. "I guess it really isn't any of my business, is it?"

"I was angry at first that you thought I was so irresponsible, but when I thought it over, I figured Carly was lucky to have a teacher who took her welfare to heart."

Was she apologizing, too? Now how the hell was he supposed to ask about Carly's apprehension every day at the end of school? "I do take her welfare to heart. She's a wonderful child, Katie."

"Thank you." She stood, script in hand. "Can I keep this?"

Adrian stood, too. "Sure. And if you want to help with rehearsals, we'll be practicing the last half hour of the day from now until show time."

"With all my experience playing Christmas angels, I'm sure I'll be a big help." Katie laughed.

Adrian liked the sound of it. He also liked the look of her when she laughed. Or when she didn't for that matter. "I'm sure you will."

Adrian had lunch duty that week so he got to watch Carly then, too. She was always the one everybody saved a seat for. She shared her cookies with the other girls at her table. Cookies that were homemade. She even gave him one on Wednesday. A lemon one with frosting on it. It was so tender it practically disappeared in his mouth before he could swallow it.

Twice, when she unwrapped her sandwich, notes fell out that said, "I hope you are having a fun day, love, Mom." The sandwiches were on homemade bread.

For the rest of the week, Katie came to school early to help with rehearsals but by Friday, Adrian still wasn't sure how he was going to pull the thing together. As the last of the kids filed out to the bus, Katie began picking up the costumes she had been trying on the kids.

Adrian watched her folding the clothes so precisely, placing them neatly in the box she had brought. It was hard to rectify that picture with the memory of her living room, with its one chair and junk leaning against the walls. Something didn't fit. It was a mystery he would never solve unless he got to know her better. Got invited back into that house. Got her talking—about something besides kids and costumes.

"You've really helped a lot, Katie. I appreciate it. If you're not busy tonight, why don't I take you and Carly out for dinner?"

Katie straightened up from folding the costumes. Adrian was leaning negligently against his desk, but she could see a line of tension in him, as if it had not been easy for him to ask her. As if he were afraid she would refuse. She wasn't sure what to answer because she wasn't sure just what he was asking. Did he just want to pay her back for her help, or did he want more than that?

Most teachers would have just sent a note. And maybe a small gift, she thought. Potholders, or a refrigerator magnet. Adrian didn't seem the potholder type. Maybe roses. Or dinner out.

She started to accept, then considered his circumstances. He couldn't have much money on a substitute teacher's pay.

Before she knew what she was doing, the words were out of her mouth. "I have a crock pot full of stew waiting at home."

With one finger, he stirred the pencils stuck into a painted juice can pencil holder, a project from earlier in the school year. A similar one Carly had made was sitting on Katie's desk at home. He looked at her from under a pair of eyebrows that were cocked lopsidedly. "Is that a gentle way of saying no, or is it an invitation?"

"Oh! An invitation, of course." She could feel herself blushing and his eyes seemed to follow that blush right down to her scoop neckline.

"I'd like to accept but I'm supposed to be treating you, remember?" It seemed to take him a minute to pull his eyes back up to her face.

The fiery blush she had felt spreading down her neck seemed to heat her very blood. "It would be a treat to have you. It's impossible to make a small pot of stew. If you help us eat some of it, we won't have to eat leftovers for three days." She was babbling. She shut up.

He chuckled. It was deep and vibrant. She could see his throat move with the sound. "I'll still owe you. How about if I help you with that stew tonight, and tomorrow night I'll take you and Carly out?"

She smiled and acquiesced, unable to see how she could graciously refuse. Her gaze wandered from his neck down to his chest, strong looking under his jersey. She wondered if he was as tanned all over as he was on the face and neck.

"What time?" he asked.

"Five? Bring your swim suit." Good Lord! What was wrong with her today? Her thoughts didn't usually jump out of her head directly into her mouth like that. "I mean, if you'd like to." Then she grinned. "You can guard Carly while I finish up the supper."

"It would be my pleasure." His gaze made a quick trip down her body and back up to her face. "Especially if you can join us for a while."

Chapter Four

ALL THE WAY HOME, AND WHILE SHE PEELED APPLES FOR A pie, Katie wondered just what she had gotten herself into. Adrian seemed to want more than to just pay her back for her help. He wanted a relationship. But did she?

It had been almost three years since Brent died. She had grieved. She missed him, but she was ready to get on with life. But was Adrian the man she wanted to get on with life with?

Well, wasn't that what the dating process was for? To find out about each other? And no matter how it had come about or how he had phrased it, this was a date.

She had wanted to find out more about Carly's teacher. Now she had the perfect opportunity. It wasn't like she was going to walk down the aisle with him next week.

She took two of the frozen balls of pie dough she kept on hand and thawed them in the microwave while she finished cutting up the apples, added flour, sugar, a dash of cinnamon, and nutmeg.

She had wondered about Mr. Adrian Wright. He was attractive enough to be a model for one of those catalogs selling sport clothes. He was lean, black-haired, and had a look in his dark eyes that told every woman who gazed into them they hid some secret only she could unearth.

Adrian's smile was infectious, especially now that he had quit scowling at her. He was kind to children, and he put himself whole-heartedly into whatever he was doing. But he was old enough to be established in a steady job. Why was he substitute teaching? How could he even live on a substitute teacher's pay?

Could he really afford to take her out? Maybe that was why he seemed so tense when he asked her.

She rolled out one of the balls of dough and put it into her biggest pie pan, a deep ten inch one, and dumped in the apples. She eyed the second ball of dough wondering what kind of top to put on the pie. Lattice? Cut out leaves and layer them all over the top? A design of an apple tree branch with leaves?

The door bell rang and she heard Carly banging the blinds to look out the window. "It's Mr. Wright, Mom," Carly called.

"Open the door for him, Honey." So much for fancy. Plain would have to do. She was rolling out the crust when Carly shepherded Adrian into the kitchen, hanging onto his hand and bouncing along in her yellow *Winnie the Pooh* swimsuit.

Adrian smiled and started to say something when he saw what she was doing. "A pie? From scratch? You didn't have to go to so much trouble," he said. But the gleam in his eyes told her he was glad.

"No trouble. I had some dough already made up and in the freezer."

"Look what Mr. Wright brought, Mommy!" Carly held up a bottle that looked a lot like champagne but which Katie could see was really a non-alcoholic sparkling grape juice. "He said we could all have some since it really isn't wine."

"Why don't you put it in the refrigerator?" Katie paused in her pie making. "Thanks, Adrian."

He was leaning against the other side of the counter, his long lean hands resting on the edge. Graceful hands, yet strong looking.

Her gaze traveled up his arms, the muscles and veins clearly outlined beneath the taut flesh. Her gaze continued traveling upward feasting on the lean maleness of him, until her greedy gaze was sabotaged by his covering shirt sleeve.

"Did you bring your swimsuit?" she asked.

Quickly, she busied herself with the pie dough, not wanting to seem like she wanted him out of his clothes so she could see the rest of him. Which was exactly what she wanted, but hated to admit. Even to herself.

He held up a pair of red trunks rolled in a towel.

"Hurry and get changed, Mr. Wright. I'll show you how good I can dive."

"Will you be joining us, Katie?"

Katie thought Adrian's voice sounded slightly husky and she realized that he wanted to see her in a swim suit every bit as much as she wanted to see him. She nodded, her throat suddenly too dry to speak. She swallowed. "I'll just finish up the pie. The bathroom is straight down the hall. You can change there."

Adrian looked at her one more time, one brow traveling speculatively upward before he went to change. Was it only her imagination that the look he gave her was almost a leer of anticipation, a mirror of her own feelings? She shook her head. He wasn't necessarily thinking the same thing she was.

She finished rolling out the top crust, put it on the pie and fluted the edges. Then, unable to resist some kind of special touch, she cut out some leaf shapes, made veins with the back of a knife and placed them along the edge of the pie.

By the time she had cleaned up the counter top and set the table, Adrian was watching Carly do her famous sea otter dive. Then her dolphin dive, then her...

Katie watched them through the window. Carly held up her arms to Adrian and he obligingly threw her into the pool then jumped in after her. She came up laughing, demanding a re-play. Carly was lapping up the fatherly attention like a thirsty terrier. A kind of attention Katie couldn't give her. Carly was getting too heavy for her to toss around. Adrian was having no trouble at all. He let her climb on his shoulders and dive into the water. He gave her toss after toss.

And while Carly was enjoying the practical application of Adrian's muscles, her mother was enjoying the sight of his lean and well-toned body, his effortless, graceful use of those sleek muscles. And yes, the rest of his body was as tan as his face and neck.

She sighed. She'd better get out there. She had promised. She checked the stew quickly then went to change.

When she got out to the pool, Carly's face lit up even more. "Mommy! Come on in! Mr. Wright is teaching me to swim on my back! Wanna see?"

Carly started splashing toward her, scrambling up the steps. Katie barely had time to catch a glance of Adrian catching a glance of her. A glance which she saw turning into an outright stare before Carly pounced on her, grabbing her hands, pulling her toward the pool. She thought she even heard the beginnings of a whistle before it was quickly stifled.

She was suddenly quite glad that she had resisted Carly's urging to buy the adult-sized matching *Winnie the Pooh* suit. She had compromised by buying a matching yellow color, a one piece cut high on the legs and with a teardrop shape peephole to one side just under her right breast. She had worried that it was just a bit daring, but had bought it anyway.

As she stepped into the pool, she noticed that Adrian was still staring and she felt a warmth spread through her. *I guess I made the right choice of swim suit after all.*

"Watch, Mommy!" Carly splashed back into the pool and headed for Adrian on her back, kicking like a half-grown tadpole.

When she came within reach, Adrian scooped her up, grinning proudly at her achievement. "Wow! I don't think The Little Mermaid can swim any better!"

Carly giggled. "Do you think a shark could catch me?"

"I don't know. Let's find out." He tossed her into the water, formed his hands into wicked claws, bared his teeth and growled at her. She shrieked and headed for the end of the pool with Adrian splashing along behind her, purposely just barely not catching her until she was almost out of the pool. Then he grabbed her, tickling and pretending to eat her while Carly laughed and tried halfheartedly to wriggle out of his arms.

Finally, she managed to "escape" and swam as fast as she could toward Katie with the "shark" right behind her. Katie enfolded her daughter protectively into her arms and turned away from the shark attack, half expecting Adrian to attack both of them, and disappointed when he didn't.

Adrian stopped his shark-claw-hand just an inch short of Katie's shoulder, and it took all his considerable will not to touch that smooth, golden shoulder with skin that looked as smooth and soft as a peach.

He was surprised at just how much he wanted to touch it, and more. It was a wanting so fierce it twisted his guts. But he forced himself to drop his hand and back away. The groan he gave was not completely fake.

"Even the toughest shark knows not to tangle with a momma mermaid," he said.

Carly wriggled free of Katie's arms and swam away from her, glancing at Adrian, inviting another chase. He was about to oblige when he heard a phone ring. Carly splashed to the steps and scrambled out of the pool, heading for a mailbox that stuck up in the middle of some bushes. She opened the mailbox, pulled out a phone and answered it.

Adrian glanced quizzically at Katie.

She shrugged and grinned. "T-mail."

"T-mail?"

"Telephone-mail," she explained. "The mailbox keeps the outdoor phone dry and protected."

Carly held one hand over the phone's mouthpiece and called, "Mom, Mr. Hoffsteder wants to know if he can borrow our grill."

"Sure. Tell him to come on over and get it."

Carly's nose wrinkled as if she suddenly smelled some foul odor. She spoke into the phone again and then hung up.

"He's coming right now," Carly said with an unhappy grimace.

"Will you unlatch the gate for him?"

Carly nodded and pattered toward the side of the house.

Moments later she returned with the tall, Nordic muscleman Adrian had seen hustling Katie up against the ladder the past Friday. Instantly, Adrian's hackles rose and he felt his hands ball into fists. It was all he could do to keep from growling.

Whoa! he told himself. *She's not your woman, you're not a caveman, and this really isn't your territory to protect.* Then he glanced at Carly. Mr. Hoffsteder was patting her awkwardly on the head and Carly skipped ahead to avoid his touch. Well, maybe it was his territory. This cretin just didn't know he was trespassing.

Mr. Hoffsteder glanced at Adrian, gave an arrogant, lopsided smile and managed to pat Carly one more time, as if to stake his claim and dare Adrian to gainsay him.

Adrian's teeth clenched. The fool seemed to think Adrian was the trespasser. He wished he could put his arm around Katie's shoulder and wave the legal papers that gave him a right to Carly under the idiot's nose. Or even better, punch it.

Katie had moved to the side of the pool with her arms braced along the edge. "Mitch, I'd like you to meet Carly's teacher, Adrian

Wright. Adrian, my neighbor, Mitch Hoffsteder."

Adrian managed a barely civil nod, but he didn't scramble out of the pool to offer his hand.

"The grill's against the house," Katie said, climbing out of the pool.

With each step higher out of the water, as more and more of Katie was revealed, Mitch's eyes grew bigger. Adrian thought the man was going to start drooling. His gaze seemed to fasten onto that same teardrop shaped hole that had so tantalized Adrian.

Adrian couldn't blame the man for his interest, or his reaction. He felt the same way. But Adrian still didn't want Mitch hanging around playing peek-a-boo with that hole. He didn't want him borrowing Katie's grill, he didn't want him next door, and he didn't want him having the right to even come into this yard when Adrian had so few rights here at all.

Carly dodged yet another pat and cannonballed into the pool, splashing water on Mitch. He yelped and looked down at his perfectly pressed khakis, ineffectually brushing at the water spots.

"Carly!" Katie gave her daughter a reproving frown.

Carly shrugged and gave Mitch a too-sweet-not-at-all-sorry smile. "I'm sorry, Mr. Hoffsteder."

Adrian could barely suppress a grin. She was on his side. A little more territory gained. Adrian wanted to "high five" Carly and say, "Good job!"

"It's all right, Katie. It's just water." Mitch was smiling but Adrian could almost hear his teeth grinding.

"The grill is next to the chimney." Katie started toward the grill and Mitch gave Adrian a last triumphant look, jauntily cocking one brow before he turned to follow Katie, his gaze gravitating to her rump.

Katie grabbed the handles of the grill and was struggling to wrest it out of the corner where it was stored. Mitch stepped up close behind her, placing one hand on hers and the other on her waist.

"Here, Sugar, let me help."

Adrian shot up out of the pool like a ballistic missile aimed right at the noisome neighbor.

Mitch's "help" was more in the line of hindrance and fondling, his "efforts" making no headway at all except to get his nose nestled into Katie's hair and his hand dangerously close to that hole.

"Here, let me give you a hand," Adrian said blithely, shouldering against Mitch to nudge him out of the way and come between Katie and her neighbor. They both moved out of the way. Adrenaline flowing, Adrian easily dislodged the grill, turned it and pushed it a few feet along the path toward the gate.

"It's all yours, Mitch," Adrian said stepping back from the grill and directly in front of Katie, shielding her from being ogled or manhandled any further, whether she wanted to be or not.

The two men eyed each other, taking each other's measure. Mitch had the advantage of height and seemed to know it, straightening himself and holding his head high.

Adrian was slightly more muscled, muscles gained from growing up hauling all day at the reins of a tough-mouthed cow pony and rescuing calves from cactus patches and ravines.

Mitch gave his lopsided grin again and leaned around Adrian to wave good-bye to Katie. He at least had brains enough to know when to back off. He was vanquished from the field for now, but his cocky grin told Adrian that he knew he had one more advantage—proximity. When the school year was over, and Adrian was out of Katie's life, Mitch would still be her neighbor.

Adrian grinned back just as cocky. Let the fool believe this was only a temporary set back. Adrian knew he still had an ace to play. One he would use when he was ready and not before. One that would keep him in Katie's life for a long time. Carly.

They went back into the pool then and let Carly practice swimming back and forth between them on her back. They swam a few laps themselves and stood in a circle with Carly batting a ball around. Carly wanted to play shark attack again but when Katie heard Adrian's stomach growl, she decided it was time to feed the mermaids and the shark some supper.

While Katie and Carly showered and dressed, Adrian swam some laps, working off some of the tension that had built higher every time he got a glimpse of that peek-a-boo hole.

He wondered just how friendly Katie was with Mr. Mitch "Muscleman" Hoffsteder. It was obvious that Carly didn't particularly like the man, but with a woman, it was harder to tell. Katie didn't seem to enjoy the liberties the man took with her. But was she, as he had first thought, man hunting?

He couldn't blame a young widow like Katie for wanting to get married again, but he'd have a thing or two to say if she got tangled up with someone who played up to Carly just for a chance to hit on her mother. Adrian angrily lashed out at the water, stroking efficiently to one end of the pool, turning and kicking off to swim the length of it underwater.

Well, hell. Wasn't that just what he was doing himself? He came up spluttering, slinging water from hair and eyes. No, actually, he was hitting on Katie to get a chance to be with Carly. Since he had learned of her existence, he had decided to be a father to her in some way. Even if it was anonymously and from afar.

Now that he had gotten to know her, he wanted more. He didn't just want the privilege of seeing her occasionally. He wanted the right—the legal right—to see her all the time, watch her grow, tuck her in at night. Every night.

She was fast becoming an addiction and the school year was fast coming to an end. Adrian leaned back against the wall of the pool and watched pink crepe myrtle flowers drift into the pool from a nearby bush. He was going to have to make a decision about Carly soon. His lawyer had assured him he would have no trouble winning legal custody. He just hoped, for Carly's sake, that it didn't have to come to that.

After supper, which they ate outside by the pool, Carly went in to watch *The Little Mermaid* video. Adrian sat content, his belly comfortably lined with stew, thick slabs of homemade bread, and two pieces of apple pie.

Adrian could see his daughter through the window sitting Indian-style in front of the TV. There was still no furniture in the living room but he was too content right then to ask why.

What more could a man ask than this, Adrian wondered. His daughter healthy and apparently happy, a good meal, a peaceful setting and a beautiful woman beside him. What more could he want? To be sure that the woman wasn't an irresponsible lush, for one thing. He frowned, remembering the smell of rum on Katie just a few days before, and the cases of beer she bought.

He glanced over at Katie. The setting sun cast a rosy glow over her, lighting her cotton candy hair to pale strawberry, and giving her a golden glow. He wondered if she was going to offer him a beer or a rum and coke, or if she preferred to try keeping her drinking a secret from her daughter's teacher. Hell, how could she drink and stay so healthy looking? Maybe she was a binge drinker? Maybe it was a healthy diet. For an impromptu meal, it had sure been quite a spread.

Maybe she wasn't a drinker at all? The thought niggled at him. What real evidence did he have, anyway? None. But finding out was as good an excuse as any to get to know Katie better—and Carly.

The sun was slowly sinking and Adrian knew it was time to go.

He still had to drive up to Austin. He had promised his mother he would help out with some ranch work tomorrow and his brother needed him to go over some company papers. He'd have to get an early start in the morning in order to get back here to take Katie and Carly out to dinner.

He stretched and stood up, dishes in hand. "Let me help you with these," he said, "then I really need to get going."

"Thanks," she said and began gathering the rest. It took two trips to carry everything into the kitchen but when Adrian started to run water into the sink, Katie protested.

"You did the cookin', ma'am. It's only right I should help clean up."

She shook her head. "The official policy in this house is that the first time you come, you're a guest and don't do dishes. The next time you come, you're family and you help out."

She took the dish cloth from his hand and their fingers brushed, sending a rush into Adrian's loins. She froze, her breath caught, and her face, even in the glare of florescent lighting, turned the same rosy color it had been outside in the setting sun. Quickly she turned away, busying herself stacking dishes by the sink.

She stood so close to him he could smell the fragrance of her shampoo, see each fine silver thread of hair. He could swear he could hear her heart thumping. Or was it his?

He lifted a hand and this time he did not pull back but laid it gently on her shoulder. His fingers glided over skin so soft it should only be allowed on babies' bottoms, and he felt her shudder, heard her quick, indrawn breath.

"Does that mean there'll be a next time?" he asked, breathing his words softly into her hair, watching it move, wanting to feel it with his lips, taste it, taste her.

She turned then and stood so close he could easily have encircled her in his arms. But there was no invitation in her stance.

She was up against the sink and couldn't back away from him, and there was tension there. He backed up, giving her space and she relaxed.

"Tomorrow night," she answered. "You're taking us out, re-member?"

It was an invitation to go. Maybe he had started to move too fast. Maybe she wasn't interested in anything more than a casual acquaintance with Carly's teacher.

He smiled and walked over to pick up his wet swim suit and towel. "Tomorrow night, then. And then I'll be family."

She laughed. But she didn't know just how much family he already was.

Chapter Five

WHEN ADRIAN RANG THE DOORBELL AT KATIE'S THE NEXT night, Carly again opened the door for him. But this time she jumped up into his arms, flinging hers around his neck.

Her hair was loose tonight, black and straight and silky, and hanging to her waist. It was held back on each side by red barrettes that matched her blouse. But Adrian could not have cared less what color she was wearing. She was in his arms at last, hugging him tight, and he had to hold himself in check to keep from squeezing her sweet little insides out.

She leaned back in his arms. "Where are we going? I told Mommy we might go to a pizza place. I said I thought you probably like pizza. But Mommy said you would probably want to go to a steakhouse." She wrinkled her nose at that.

Adrian had a hard time keeping a serious look on his face. "I never even considered going to a steakhouse. Pizza was all I could think of." Then he leaned closer. "Your mom does like pizza, doesn't she?"

"She loves it!" Carly wiggled to get down and he let her slide to the floor.

"What do I love?" Katie asked as she came into the room.

"Pizza!" Carly said, "We're going to get pizza!"

"She managed to talk you into pizza, huh?" Katie looked askance at her daughter, but a smile played at the corners of her mouth. "Yeah, and it didn't take very long at all. Must have learned those feminine wiles from you." Adrian knew he was staring, but he couldn't help himself. He was as bad as Mitch What's-his-name. Worse. Katie had done something with her hair, put it up some way that looked like it would all come tumbling down if he could just find the one key pin holding it all together.

And he wasn't sure she should be allowed out of the house in the outfit she wore. The soft blue silky top wasn't tight at all, but it clung to her in places and left too much to the imagination where it didn't cling. And that skirt might be long and full, but it swirled around, brushing calves, clinging to thighs, gliding over hips, nipping in at her waist in an open invitation to hands to touch, and circle.

She even smelled good. He breathed in deeply. Even from all the way across the room he could smell... "Cake?"

Katie laughed. "I just took a carrot cake out of the oven. I thought we could come back here for dessert."

Cake. Better than perfume, he thought. "Great. All ready?"

He took them to an Italian restaurant instead of a pizza parlor. But he made sure pizza was on the menu. He ordered one himself with banana peppers and sesame seeds around the edge. Katie went with fettuccini Alfredo and Carly dove into the Italian Medley pizza—loaded with everything.

The waitress came back to check on them and watched Carly down bite after bite, black olives, onions, mushrooms and all. "Not a fussy eater, is she?"

"Not at all," Katie answered.

The waitress looked at Adrian's plate, already half empty. "Takes after her father, I guess."

"Looks just like you, too," the waitress said to Adrian. "You can't deny this one." She picked up Katie's empty salad plate. "You folks enjoy your meal now."

Adrian froze, wondering what to say, wondering what Katie would say.

There was a long silence. Too long. "I'm sorry," Katie said at last.

Sorry? Adrian wasn't sorry. He was suddenly so full of himself he could hardly stand it. The waitress thought Carly looked like him. Sorry? Only because he couldn't tell the whole world that she was his. Sorry? Only because he was afraid Katie would figure out who he was before he was ready to tell her.

Adrian shrugged, trying to make it seem casual. "It's a perfectly natural mistake."

"I guess it is. You two do look alike." Katie studied each of them while Adrian's blood ran cold. As cold as his now forgotten pizza was getting. "Same coloring, same eyes. It's amazing. Are you part Native American, Adrian?"

The banana pepper and sesame seeds seemed permanently stuck in his throat. He looked down at his plate where he had unconsciously started shredding what was left of his pizza and took a drink of Coke.

"Yeah. I am." He said it almost defensively. He had faced prejudice before and was ready to face it again. But Katie just nodded.

"I've often wondered if Carly has some in her." Katie was playing absently with her food, too, making four trails through the Alfredo sauce with her fork.

Adrian thought he was going to choke.

"Oh!" Katie looked up at his expression. "Carly is adopted."

"Really?" was all Adrian managed to croak out.

"I hope you weren't embarrassed, but it's kind of nice, actually, to have someone think Carly really belongs to me without any suspicion. Brent was blond like me and when we would all go out together, people were more likely to ask us where she got her dark hair and eyes, and give me an arch look like I must have fooled around."

Adrian squirmed.

"Sorry. I didn't mean to get so personal. I'm sure you don't want to hear this."

Adrian glanced at Carly who had finished her pizza and was blithely coloring her menu with the three crayons the restaurant had given her. "Does Carly know?"

"That she's adopted? Yes. We never kept it a secret from her or anyone."

Adrian nodded, relieved. It would make things easier when... if...

Katie laughed, a little strained, but a laugh. "Frankly, I've often wondered myself where Carly got her dark hair and eyes. The adoption agency tries to match the children with the adoptive parents as much as possible. They told us that her mother was blond and that the father, although he was unknown, was probably blond as well." Katie shrugged lightly. "I guess he wasn't after all."

Adrian looked down into his lap, creasing and smoothing his napkin. "No, I guess he wasn't."

Back at Katie's, Adrian sat on the living room floor and played *Chutes and Ladders* with Carly, while Katie brewed some coffee and set out plates and forks.

When the game was done, they had their cake at the kitchen table and Adrian thought it would not be hard at all to get used to this—to having dinner with his daughter every night, playing games on the living room floor, finishing the evening with a piece of homemade cake.

He could easily see the three of them falling into a pattern. The questionable part was Katie. He just couldn't be sure of Katie, yet. She didn't seem like a lush, but he remembered the rum and cases of beer. She didn't seem irresponsible, but why was Carly so worried every day about whether or not Katie would show up to take her home? She didn't seem disorganized but, well, there was that living room looking like a bomb hit. But the kitchen was clean and organized, the outside well kept. It didn't add up, somehow. But as long as he could be with Carly, he was willing to stick around and find out about her adoptive mother. Especially, he thought, putting another chunk of carrot cake into his mouth, when sticking around was so pleasant.

Carly finished her milk and yawned. She looked up quickly at Katie, a glum expression on her face. "I know. Time for bed."

Katie just nodded.

"Can I stay up a while 'cause Mr. Wright's here?" Carly asked.

Katie leaned over until she was eye-to-eye with Carly, foreheads touching. "Do you really want to turn into a rattlesnake in front of your teacher?"

Carly giggled but alarm bells went off in Adrian's head. What kind of malarkey had Katie been feeding his daughter? Had she really told her she'd turn into a rattlesnake if she didn't go to bed on time?

"Okay." The word came out on a long, slow sigh of resignation. "Goodnight, Mr. Wright."

"Goodnight, Carly."

Carly got up, took her dishes to the sink and headed down the hall, dragging her feet.

As soon as she was out of earshot Adrian caught Katie's eye and asked, "Rattlesnake?"

Katie laughed lightly. "Normally, Carly is a wonderful child.

But when she gets overtired, she gets so cranky. It's like she's as nasty and biting as a rattlesnake. So we made a game of it. If she doesn't want to go to bed, or starts getting snappish, I just remind her that she's turning into a rattlesnake. She laughs and understands it's time for bed."

The knot of apprehension in Adrian's chest melted into understanding, then flared into downright admiration for Katie's parenting. He nodded approvingly. "Very clever."

Katie started to gather up the silverware but he stopped her, taking the forks from her hand and stacking Katie's plate on top of his. "I'm family now, remember? I'll wash."

Katie surrendered the silverware into his hand. "And I'll let you while I get Carly settled and read her a story. It won't take long."

Adrian just nodded, unable to speak, riddled with envy at the casual way she headed down the hall to read Carly a story and tuck her in. He would have jumped at the chance to do it. Begged her for the privilege, even, if it wouldn't have seemed a bit strange.

Instead, he was stuck with the dishes. Well, there weren't many and he was finished by the time Katie returned.

"All tucked in?" he asked.

"All tucked in," she affirmed. "Would you like to sit here in the kitchen or out by the pool? It's pleasant out there and I'm afraid the living room is..." She waved her hand in a gesture that was more frustration than helplessness.

Adrian cocked an eyebrow toward the living room. "I had wondered about that."

She laughed lightly. "I sent the furniture out to get reupholstered. The painter was supposed to be here last week so I took down all the pictures and boxed up the knick-knacks. But he had some family emergency and had to postpone. He's promised me he'll be here Monday morning and I sure hope so because the furniture will be back on Thursday. And I'm getting tired of living in what looks like a war zone."

With a long "aaah" of understanding, relief eased into Adrian's mind and, mentally, he inched a bit closer to accepting that, perhaps, he had seen Katie with a jaundiced eye. Perhaps he had been looking for faults, excuses...no, reasons, to proclaim her unfit to be his child's mother. And maybe even a few to keep from finding her quite so attractive. "So that explains it."

She gave a shrugging nod and headed toward the double glass doors that led to the pool. Adrian followed, reaching around her to open the door. He held the knob just a moment, taking in the scent of her, reveling in the feel of her half way into his embrace, wanting more, holding back, making his mind take charge of his impulses. He had to remember why he was here—to get to know Carly. Katie had stayed single for three years. Maybe she wanted to stay that way. He didn't want to jeopardize his welcome in this house by moving in on Katie too fast, no matter how physically attractive she was. And she was gut-wrenchingly attractive.

She had taken her hair down. It formed a silver halo about her head and shoulders, and the moonlight on it gave it a glow. Golden in the sunlight, silver in the shadows, he thought. It was not going to be easy to sit in the moonlight with her and just talk.

She pulled a chair up next to another one and sat down, inviting him, with a wave of her hand, to sit. He settled into the padded patio chair and stretched out his legs. Her feet were a hairsbreadth from his. Her hand dangled over the arm of her chair mere inches away. The sun had just set, birds were settling in for the night, crickets were chirping, and a soft breeze flowed over them.

Carly. He was here for Carly. And he wanted to know all there was to know about his daughter. Every cute thing, every naughty thing, every clever thing she had ever done.

He cleared his throat and tried to sound casual when he asked,

"How old was Carly when you got her?"

The underwater light was on in the pool and he could see Katie's face clearly. She seemed surprised at his question. As if she had expected their conversation to take a different tack. Or was he asking too many questions about Carly? Was she beginning to get suspicious of him?

But she shrugged nonchalantly when she answered, "Two weeks old," and he was encouraged to probe further, to try to get her talking.

"I'll bet she was a cutie."

That was all it took. Katie loved her adopted daughter and if someone wanted to hear about her, she was happy to reminisce. "Cute and sweet and wonderful. Round and fat and happy. Her skin was so smooth and soft." Katie laughed. "Well, I guess most babies have smooth, soft skin, don't they?"

Adrian joined in her laughter. It was easy to do. He was feeling so good sitting here hearing about Carly. "But Carly's was extra smooth and soft, right?"

"Of course!"

"So, she was a good baby?"

"We couldn't have asked for better. Of course her toddler days were a bit rough at times." Katie chuckled. "One day when she was about two I had to make a cake for St. Patrick's Day. So, I made green and white cake batter, made a ring with foil in the pan and poured the layers so that when you cut the cake, it would be a checkerboard design. I put it in the oven and just a few minutes later, there was smoke pouring out of the oven and the cake was burning."

"You sure you didn't just leave it in too long?"

"Nope. It had just been fifteen minutes and I had charcoal. I noticed that the oven temperature was set on five hundred and twenty five degrees. I couldn't figure out how I could have done something so stupid. Well, I mixed up another cake, put it in the oven, set the timer, and made sure the temperature was right. A couple of minutes later I found out what had happened to the first cake. I turned around and there was Carly, up on the counter, playing with the temperature controls!"

Adrian laughed. "I guess she wanted to bake, too."

"That wasn't the end of it. When I took the cake out of the oven, I decided not to let a warm oven go to waste so I mixed up a batch of yogurt. Basically, I had about two quarts of sour milk. You put that into a warm oven, turn off the oven and the yogurt sets overnight. I was washing up some dishes when all of a sudden I heard the oven door open, and before I could stop her, Carly grabbed the dish and said, 'What's dat, Mom?' just before the sour milk spilled all over the oven, on the floor, and into the oven drawer." Katie shook her head. "Carly went to bed a bit early that night."

"And not too happy about it, either, I guess."

"She did get a good talking to," Katie said, laughing, "mainly about hot ovens and safety."

Katie's laughter died down to a soft smile. "She's a very special person. And very special to me."

A spear of guilt twisted itself into Adrian's gut. Even if he found out that Katie did have a problem with alcohol, that there was a sound reason why Carly grew apprehensive when it was time for Katie to pick her up, could he really take her daughter away from her?

He knew enough about Katie now that one thing was certain, she had been a good mother to Carly, or Carly would not be the happy, well-adjusted kid he saw. But if he didn't take Carly, where did that leave him? An hour away in Austin seeing his daughter, at best, every other weekend? That wasn't good enough. Not for him.

There was another alternative. He could marry Katie. But that would be a heck of a thing to do just to have a right to see his own kid. Marriage should be based on more than that. Well, he was very physically attracted to Katie. But could he marry a woman he had known only two weeks? A woman he still had misgivings about?

He certainly didn't want to drag Carly and Katie through the courts. Even if his lawyer had assured him he would have no trouble winning. He might win, but Katie would have to lose. And what about Carly? Would she win or lose? What was best for her? He still didn't know.

His brother had advised him to give this some time. So far, Jace had been right. He had had a lot of his misgivings about Katie allayed. Maybe he could get to know them both well enough that all his misgivings would be resolved and he could take the easy route to Carly. Marry her mother.

But he couldn't think about this any more tonight. He was bone-tired from his workout at the ranch that had started before sunup. He still had a pile of papers from the family oil company to go over, and he had to get away from Katie before he made a move on her that she might not be ready for.

He stretched and stood up. "I gotta go, Katie. It's getting late. Thanks for the carrot cake. It was the best I've ever had."

She stood up with him. The breeze molded her dress to her, casting her form into silver, blue, and shadows. He caught her fragrance. Vanilla and cake were part of it, and something else indefinably alluring.

It had been a long time since Adrian had been even halfway serious about a woman. A long time. Too long. And this one was unconsciously throwing out snares and lures with every breath, with each rise and fall of her chest, every sway of her breasts and hips. The moonlight didn't help. Adrian was suddenly very glad he had worn a pair of loose khakis. Tight jeans would have been a dead giveaway.

"Would you like a piece of cake to take with you?"

Hell, no, he didn't want to take a piece of cake with him. He wanted to take her into his arms, take her to bed and wake up here in the morning to have a piece of that carrot cake for breakfast with his daughter. And Katie.

"Sure. I'll have it for breakfast." *Alone*, he thought. *In that stupid, barren apartment. While you're over here having scrambled eggs and ham and homemade biscuits with Carly.* Damn. Marriage had never been more appealing.

He headed toward the house before he did something stupid. Like taking Katie into his arms and kissing her. Like pressing her close and seeing if his hands really would go all the way around her waist. Like filling his hands with the soft swells of her breasts.

He almost stumbled going into the house, he was in such a hurry. He flipped on the kitchen switch, and cold, white fluorescent light doused him like a cold shower.

Well, maybe not quite that effective. Not with Katie's appealingly rounded backside in front of him as she stood at the counter, cutting and wrapping a generous hunk of the cake for him.

She walked with him to the door, and, with a smile, placed the cake into his waiting hands. Hands that curled around hers, holding just a little longer than necessary. He didn't want to let go. Didn't want this to end. Wanted...had to see Carly again. And Katie.

Maybe she wasn't adverse to seeing him again, either. She didn't pull her hands away. And her smile softened to a wistful look with shining eyes.

"How about if I take you and Carly to the zoo tomorrow? We can find a real Stripey Tiger for her to see, and afterward she can ride the carousel in Breckenridge Park, and we'll all take the train ride." He bit his lip to stop his own chatter. He sounded like an overeager high school boy.

She probably had plans. He hadn't thought about that. A band seemed to tighten around his chest. She probably had family to see. The band squeezed harder. And friends. Harder. Shopping to do. He could scarcely breathe.

"I'd like that. I'm sure Carly will, too."

Adrian blinked. She accepted. Just like that. He was going to see them again tomorrow. The band broke and he had breath and life again.

"Great. I'll pick you up about two, okay?"

She nodded and before he lost his nerve, before he let go of her hands, he bent and gave her the quickest, barest kiss possible on the cheek. Then before she could slap him or tell him she had changed her mind, he was out the door and into his car, driving away.

Chapter Six

FOR THE LONGEST TIME, KATIE STOOD THERE STARING AFTER Adrian. She could still feel the faint brush of his lips on her cheek, the warmth of his hands cradling hers, the crinkled roughness of the aluminum foil that had wrapped the cake.

Slowly she closed the door and leaned her forehead against it. This was definitely not the average parent-teacher relationship. He wanted much more from her than the typical thank you note and box of note cards at the end of the school year next week.

Still feeling the tingle in her cheek, she lifted her head and locked the door, went to the kitchen, turned out the light, and headed down the hall to her bedroom. Her empty bedroom and lonely bed. She wanted more, too.

She turned back the light comforter and sheet and stood looking down at the bed. When Brent had died, she had cocooned herself with Carly. She gave Carly all her time and attention, reading to her, taking her to museums, teaching her to swim, to play soccer and board games.

Then Carly had gone to school and Katie had realized that she could not depend on her daughter to fill the emotional void. There had been a few dates. But the men had either been quickly put off by the idea of taking on a child as well as a woman, or she had quickly seen that they were only being marginally nice to Carly to keep Katie's interest.

She had heard enough horror stories about step parents to want to be very careful who she got involved with. Even if it meant not getting involved at all until Carly was grown. She had heard a lot of good stories, too, and that kept her going, trying, but until Adrian came along two weeks ago, she hadn't found anyone she wanted to pursue beyond that first date.

It had been pleasant being mistaken for a family at the restaurant. It had been more than pleasant being with Adrian. It was nice being with a man who seemed to really care about Carly. Who didn't just play up to the daughter to impress the mother.

In fact, sometimes it seemed that he was more interested in Carly than her. Well, he certainly loved kids.

Katie took off her clothes, put on a nightgown and slipped between the cool, smooth sheets, feeling the loneliness more than she had in a long time. She ran a hand over the neighboring pillow, easily imagining Adrian there.

She wished he hadn't kissed her. It had been a simple kiss, almost chaste. But it had stirred longings in her she had tried too long to suppress. Feelings that were not hard to suppress around most of the men she had dated in the last three years. With Adrian it had been hard to suppress them from the very first time Carly had introduced him as "Mr. Right."

Well, maybe he was "Mr. Right." Maybe he was just who she wanted, just who she needed. Just who Carly needed.

Or maybe her hormones were moving too fast.

She punched her pillow and flopped over. There was a lot more to consider than the fact that he liked kids and had a great body. Like the fact that she knew nothing about him except that he was Carly's substitute teacher.

He was awfully good at being goofy with Carly and making

her laugh. He was awfully good at asking his own questions. But she suddenly realized that he had told her absolutely nothing about himself.

When they had gone to the restaurant tonight and he had opened the door to his car for her, she had been surprised to be ushered into a late model Lexus. She wasn't sure what she had expected, maybe an old Chevy, but she certainly hadn't expected a substitute teacher to be tooling around in a Lexus.

"Nice car," she had commented.

"Thanks," was all he had said before changing the topic back to her. "I like that red sports car of yours, too. It surprised me that first day I met you. I expected Carly to be picked up in a station wagon or mini van. Why did you choose a car like that?"

She had laughed, easily diverted. Too easily. "It was my husband's. I guess I've just held onto it for sentimental reasons."

He had nodded as if a deep mystery had just been explained and then asked Carly what she liked best on pizza.

Katie punched her pillow. So, where did a substitute teacher get the money to buy a Lexus? For that matter, what was a man Adrian's age doing substituting? Shouldn't he be established in some career by now? Those were unsettling questions that had to be answered before she could let herself be drawn into a deeper relationship. No matter what her body was telling her, no matter what her instincts told her, no matter what her daughter's laughter told her, she had to at least pay some attention to her brain.

The next time she saw Adrian, she was determined to get some answers.

But the next day at the zoo and the park, Katie had no chance to ask Adrian personal questions. Carly launched into him the moment she saw him coming up the walk. And he seemed content to let her nearly monopolize his time and attention.

Halfway up the walk he scooped Carly up and threw her over

one shoulder, winking broadly at Katie as he carried Carly into the house. "Look what I found! A monkey escaped from the zoo. I think we'd better take it back."

Carly had shrieked delightedly at being thrown over Adrian's shoulder but when she started to protest over being called a monkey, he tickled her and she squirmed and giggled.

"Not a monkey, huh?" Adrian asked, tickling some more. "Then why are you chattering like one?"

Adrian set Carly down when he saw Katie struggling to the door with a huge cooler. He took it from her. "What's this?"

Katie shrugged, glad to be relieved of the heavy weight, admiring the easy way he handled it. "We're going to the park. I thought a picnic lunch would be a good idea."

Adrian's brows shot up and his eyes lit appreciatively, roving briefly over her, warming her more than the sun. "Sounds like a wonderful idea to me. That was really thoughtful of you, Katie. Thanks."

Adrian hustled the cooler out to the car and put it in the trunk. Then he opened the back door for Carly and the front door for Katie, touching her lightly on the arm, and setting off a flood of sensations she shouldn't be having in broad daylight.

At the zoo, Adrian paid their entrance fee then set Carly on his shoulders to carry her. The first thing they saw were the flamingos.

"Phew! They stink!" said Carly.

Adrian tugged one of Carly's legs. "I thought that was this little monkey."

"I'm not a monkey," Carly protested, laughing.

Adrian hauled her around to peer intently into her face. "Hmm. She does look familiar. What do you think, Katie? Monkey or little girl?"

"Big girl," Carly corrected.

"Big girl," Adrian conceded.

Katie grinned at his tomfoolery, enjoying it as much, maybe more, than Carly. "I think I've seen her around."

"Hmm. Well, I guess we'd better find the monkeys and see if anyone there recognizes her."

When they came to a sign directing visitors to various areas of the zoo, Adrian paused as if puzzling over the direction. "Now which way do we go?"

"That way," Carly said. She pointed emphatically down one path.

"That way?" Adrian asked. He pointed a different direction altogether.

"No! That way!" Carly pointed again, leaning over and tugging Adrian's hair.

"Ah! This way!" Adrian started off down the wrong path.

Carly kicked her heels against Adrian's chest and tugged his hair harder. "No, no! That way!"

Adrian pulled Carly off his shoulders and set her down. "I guess you're just going to have to lead the way." She took his hand and reached for Katie's with the other and hauled them along toward the monkeys. She skipped happily along between them like any child with both parents in tow and Katie thought how nice it was having someone holding Carly's other hand. Holding, even for an afternoon, some of the responsibility for this child. Sometimes they lifted her up high, swinging her between them as she skipped, and she begged them to do it again and again until Katie's arm ached.

At last they found the monkeys and Carly turned to Adrian, arms uplifted in silent expectation to be held up to see. Adrian again lifted Carly up to his shoulders.

"Hey, any of you guys recognize this monkey I found?" Adrian called. The monkeys blithely ignored them. Going from one exhibit to the next, Adrian pretended to show Carly off as if to ask if any of the apes knew her.

Adrian sighed. "They don't recognize her. Think we're going to have to keep her, Katie?"

Katie gave an exaggerated sigh, but felt a warmth at Adrian's use of the word "we." "I guess so."

Adrian started to put Carly down but she clung to him. "Carry me. Please."

"Carly, I think you can walk for a while," Katie said.

"I'll carry her. I don't mind."

"Really, Adrian, you don't have to carry her all the time," Katie said, not wanting Carly to impose on Adrian's goodwill, or wear it out.

"My pleasure, Ma'am." He jiggled Carly's foot, holding on to the toe of her sandal. "My pleasure."

Katie looked at the two of them, at Adrian's genuine grin, the sparkle in his eyes when he looked at Carly. He acted as if carrying Carly were one of the greatest gifts he had ever been given and though she was pleased, Katie wondered why he would feel that way about her after such a short acquaintance. Did he love kids that much?

"Okay," Katie conceded, "but don't let her wear you out."

"This little peanut?"

"Peanut?" Carly asked from overhead, as they headed down another path.

"Yeah, peanut," Adrian answered. "I thought you were a monkey but since they didn't know you I figured you're really just a little peanut. So, I'm taking you over to see if the elephant wants you."

Carly giggled. "I'm not a peanut. I'm a kid!"

Adrian leaned toward Katie, "A kid? I'm carrying around a goat?"

Katie just rolled her eyes and moved away from them as if

disavowing all knowledge of them. Adrian caught up to her and slung one arm about her shoulders, daring her to deny knowing either of them.

It was easy for Katie to lean into him, to feel comfortable to be there, for the weight of his arm across her shoulders to make her feel cared for. After the last three years of being the one totally responsible for everything in her and Carly's life, it was a good feeling, even if it was just for an afternoon.

They visited the elephant who assured Adrian that Carly was indeed not a peanut. Then they visited the tiger, comparing it toe to tail with Carly's Stripey Tiger and deciding that, except for size and friendliness, they were a lot alike.

After a quick stop to see the zebras and hippos, they all professed an avid interest in the contents of the cooler in the trunk of the car and decided to go to the park to eat.

Katie held Carly's hand while Adrian lugged the cooler to a table and they had tuna sandwiches on whole wheat homemade bread, chips, and celery sticks stuffed with peanut butter. There were slices of the carrot cake and fruit and canned fruit juice.

They all took the train ride around the park, then Carly rode the carousel. Three times. Carly begged for a fourth ride and Adrian was ready to let her but Katie called a halt.

"No more today. It's getting late," she said. "By the time we get home, get ready for school tomorrow..."

"No! I want to ride the carousal again. Mr. Wright said I could."

"Okay," Adrian said.

Katie opened her mouth to protest. What right did he have to interfere with the way she handled her daughter? But Adrian had already scooped Carly up and set her on his shoulders.

"But this is the horsie you get to ride this time." With a quick wink and a "are you coming" look to Katie he made a neighing sound and began bobbing up and down like a carousal horse and headed toward the car, a laughing Carly clinging to his hair.

Katie followed along thoughtfully, appreciative of how neatly Adrian had satisfied both of them and diffused the situation.

At home, Adrian carried in the cooler while Katie sent Carly to get her bath. With an easy swing Adrian set the cooler on the kitchen counter.

"Thanks, Adrian. And thanks for your help with Carly at the carousal. I could tell she was getting tired."

Adrian folded both arms across the top of the cooler and grinned. "I don't like 'rattlesnakes' any more than you do."

Katie laughed. "She can certainly turn into one when she gets tired."

Adrian shrugged. "Most kids will. Carly's a lot better than most I've seen."

Katie's heart warmed at his words, at his acceptance of the less pleasant side of kids. "You really love kids, don't you?"

Adrian gave a wistful, lopsided smile. "Yeah. I've always wanted a houseful."

"A houseful?"

"Well, four or five, anyway. I like big families."

Seeing her chance to find something out about Adrian without seeming to actually pry, she asked, "Do you come from a large family, Adrian?"

"There are six of us. Three boys, three girls. What about you?"

"I'm an only child. But I baby-sat a lot growing up and always thought I would have a big family." She looked down at her fingers resting on the edge of the counter remembering Brent's and her anguish over their inability to conceive a child. "It...just didn't work out that way."

"I'm sorry."

Katie shrugged. "If Brent and I could have had our own children, we wouldn't have gotten Carly, now would we?"

She pulled the cooler to her side of the counter and began unpacking it, suddenly realizing how neatly he had turned the topic back to her, again. There were still a couple of sandwiches left. She held one up to Adrian. "Want another sandwich?"

Adrian took the sandwich, unwrapped it, took a big bite, and sighed appreciatively. "Lady, you make the best bread I've ever tasted."

"Thanks." She handed him a can of juice to go along with the sandwich then shoved the second sandwich across the counter to him.

He shook his head. "This is plenty."

"Then take it for lunch tomorrow."

He picked up the wrapped sandwich and turned it over, looking closely at it. "Any notes tucked in here?"

She felt a blush spread across her face and chest. "You've seen Carly's lunches."

Adrian chuckled. "I was on lunch duty last week. She really appreciates your notes, Katie. They mean a lot to her."

"I hope so. I don't send one every day, but sometimes, I love her so much, I just can't resist."

Adrian put the wrapped sandwich back on the counter, pushed it back and forth with one finger. "I've come to realize that." He looked at the sandwich thoughtfully, the half eaten one momentarily forgotten. "Katie, do you mind if I ask you a personal question about Carly? You don't have to answer it if you don't want to."

"Go ahead." She suddenly felt like she needed to be on the defensive. It was an effort not to cross her arms.

"Carly..." He paused as if wondering how to proceed. "At the end of the day Carly gets so tensed up. She's made a couple of remarks as if she's worried that you might not show up to get her. Yet, you've never failed to be there. Can you tell me what's causing it? If there's anything I can do?"

"It's still there." Katie hadn't meant to say that out loud. She felt her own knot of tension and took a deep breath to relieve it, scrubbing both hands over her face then clasping them together tightly, interlacing her fingers and leaning against the counter just a moment. They were difficult memories.

"When Carly was three, almost four, her father was killed in a car accident. You already knew that, I think."

Adrian nodded.

"We had put Carly into a day care just one afternoon a week. We thought it would be good for her and would give me some time off, too." She unclasped her hands and placed them flat on the counter. Adrian reached across and took one in his. It helped. A lot.

"Brent was going to pick her up on his way home from work. He was driving my car that day. It had been worked on and he wanted to make sure it was okay. He never made it. He was hit by a drunk driver and killed. By the time I found out what happened and went to get her, Carly had waited a long time for a father who never showed up."

Adrian squeezed her hand. "So, when it's time to get picked up..."

"Right. She wonders if I'm going to make it. That first day I met you," she gave a little laugh, "I was cleaning out the gutters when I realized how late it was. I didn't take time to clean up."

Adrian grinned mischievously. "I remember how lovely you looked."

"I remember your expression."

"I had no right to judge."

They leaned toward each other, close enough that she could feel his breath on her cheek, against her hair, could feel the heat of his body reaching out to her.

"Mommy, can you comb my hair now?"

They jumped apart almost guiltily and turned to see Carly in the doorway, her nighties on, Stripey Tiger under one arm, her comb in one hand, and her hair a wet, tangled, mess.

Katie sat down on a kitchen chair and pulled Carly close, kissing her on top of her wet hair before she started combing out the tangles.

Adrian stood watching a moment while finishing his sandwich. He picked up the last sandwich and chucked Carly under the chin. "I'd better go. Thanks, princess, for the day at the zoo."

"Thanks, Mr. Wright."

Katie started to get up but Adrian put a hand on her shoulder. "I can let myself out. See you tomorrow?"

She nodded. He picked up his wrapped sandwich and left. Katie watched him go, wishing she had had time to put a note in his sandwich, but not sure what she would have written.

Chapter Seven

ADRIAN SHUT THE DOOR ON HIS WAY OUT OF KATIE'S, MAKING sure it locked. He glared at the keys in his hand, two car keys, the apartment key, one to his house in Austin, the office, even one each for his parents' house and his grandparents'. Just none to the door he had just locked behind him. Okay, so he had been completely wrong about Katie.

Adrian got in the car, backed out of the driveway and headed home. *Home. Yeah, right*, he thought. He would hardly call that bare, cold apartment a home. Not even the little house he had built on one corner of his grandparents' ranch seemed much like home anymore.

If home is where the heart is, then Adrian knew where his home was. He had just left it.

But he couldn't stand to stay there another minute watching Katie gently comb Carly's hair, getting her ready for bed, doing all the hundred simple little things that mothers and kids do, knowing Katie would soon be going to bed, too, and it wouldn't be with him. Knowing that he was just an outsider, not part of that pattern.

He glanced at the sandwich she had given him, lying there on the passenger seat. Like crumbs to a dog, he thought. He didn't just want a sandwich to take. He didn't want to view enticing bits of their lives and then have to leave. He wanted her to put that sandwich in her—no, their—refrigerator so it could wait there all night for him to get out of bed with her, eat breakfast with Carly, then have it for lunch. With them.

Jace had been right. He had given Katie time and a chance to prove herself and all his suspicions had turned out to be just that. Suspicions. Preconceived suspicions with no basis. He had wanted his daughter and had been looking for reasons to justify taking her. And he had found none. Katie wasn't man hunting. Mitch What's-His-Name might come on to her, but up close, Adrian had seen how uncomfortable it had made her. Katie certainly didn't seem to encourage the man.

The barren living room had been explained, Carly's end of day anxiety. Even the booze and cigarettes he had helped her put in her car that day at the grocery had been explained last night at the restaurant when the waitress had asked whether they wanted to be seated in the smoking or non-smoking section.

Adrian had looked to Katie to answer and she had said, "I'd prefer non-smoking, if that's all right with you, Adrian. I don't smoke and I don't really like Carly to be around it."

"Oh, I thought maybe you smoked since you bought cigarettes the other day."

"Those were for my neighbor. The beer and wine, too. She was having a party. She's crippled and I usually do her shopping for her."

Adrian turned into his street swearing to himself that he was going to be more trusting in the future. Especially when it came to Katie. The only thing his suspicions had gotten him so far were the beginnings of an ulcer. If he found Katie next week with a body at her feet and a smoking gun in her hand, he was going to assume she was completely innocent, ask for an explanation, and not jump to conclusions.

Trust. If he was going to think about marriage to Katie, he had to learn to trust her. And that was just what he was going to do from now on.

The last week of school was a busy one. By Tuesday the last lesson had been taught, the last papers returned, and grades turned in. Wednesday and Thursday desks were cleaned out and scrubbed, bulletin boards taken down, books collected and stored for the summer. Only one morning of school was left, the day for the awards ceremony and the first grade play.

Excitement ran high behind the curtain and Adrian had to keep telling the ninjas not to kick the curtain, and assure the queens and princesses that even though the dragons said they were breathing fire on them, it was just pretend fire and they really weren't being scorched. Katie seemed to have an endless supply of safety pins for fallen fairy wings and torn hems.

But at last the curtain was up, the play was on and only two kids forgot their lines and had to be prompted from the wings. The applause at the end was thunderous and every first grader beamed with memories they would cherish for a lifetime.

Mrs. Sandy, the first grader's teacher, had come for the performance, baby cradled in her arms and being oohed and aahed over by the girls.

Awards were given out by each teacher and Katie held Mrs. Sandy's baby while the teacher helped Adrian hand out straight-A awards, student council pins, and final report cards with "Promoted to Grade Two" on the back of each one.

From the stage Adrian could see Katie holding Mrs. Sandy's baby. Her eyes were shining and he thought he had never seen her look so happy. And that was when it struck him that if he married

Katie Simmons, he would never have that house full of children they had both dreamed about.

It was an effort to keep smiling with that wrenching thought knotting his gut. He almost dropped the last two report cards as he handed them to Mrs. Sandy to give out. He looked again at Katie, so beautiful, almost Madonna-like, holding that baby.

But he didn't have time now to think of whether or not marrying Katie would be worth giving up having more children. He had expectant faces waiting for him to give out the perfect attendance awards. Ruthlessly, he shoved his worries to the back of his mind to be dealt with later. He watched each of the kids he had gotten to know walk across that stage and out of his life. All but one. Somehow, no matter what it took, he would make sure that Carly would be a part of his life forever.

At last the awards ceremony was over, Mrs. Sandy had hugged each first grader and promised to see them next year when they were in second grade, and parents had picked up the last child. Adrian's job here was finished.

Katie was boxing up the last of the costumes and Carly had gone home with Angela.

"Thanks so much for your help, Katie," Adrian said.

"It went great, didn't it?" she responded.

"I could never have done it without you. Could I take you and Carly out for pizza tonight?"

Katie looked straight at him, a challenging look in her eyes. "Carly is spending the night with Angela."

Adrian took her challenge for exactly what it was. A question of, "Who are you really interested in, Carly or me?" And Adrian hesitated because he wasn't sure of the answer. Yes, he had thought about marrying Katie, but was it only to get Carly?

But he did know one thing. He wouldn't be able to see Carly without seeing Katie. And he had to keep seeing Carly.

He managed a grin. "Then we don't have to go to a pizza place, do we? We can go someplace else."

She seemed to let out a breath she had been holding. "I'd like that."

"So, what would you like? Chinese? Mexican? That steakhouse you were sure I'd want to go to last time?"

She laughed. "Wherever you want to go is fine."

Adrian shook his head. "I'm taking you out, remember? The choice is yours."

She bit her lip. "Well, I love Chinese but never go because Carly doesn't care for it."

"Then Chinese it is. Pick you up about six?"

At six, Adrian was ringing the doorbell and Katie was ready and waiting for him. When he opened the car door for her he realized that this was a date. A real date. Not just a thank you dinner or an excuse to be with Carly. And though the back seat seemed awfully empty and quiet, it was nice to be out with Katie alone.

"What will you do now that school is out for the summer, Adrian?"

Adrian glanced over at her, recognizing the challenge in her voice again and he suddenly wondered if she had deliberately arranged for Carly to be gone tonight, to have a chance to get some answers out of him. Until now, he had managed to evade most of her questions. With Carly along, it hadn't been hard. She took most of the attention. And when she had been put to bed, he had had his own questions to ask. Now there would be no avoiding telling Katie something about himself. Mentally, he shrugged. What harm could it do? There was only one thing he still wasn't ready to tell her—the fact that he was ninety-nine percent sure he was Carly's natural father.

"I guess I'll go back to my regular job," he answered. "In Austin." He grinned over at her. "An oil company."

"And what do you do at this oil company?"

"I own it."

She leaned away from him, narrowing her eyes suspiciously and crossing her arms, nearly causing him to go off the road at the enticing display of rounded bosom her gesture brought into his view. Her eyes narrowed and her head tilted. "So you're a big Texas oil man?"

With an almost apologetic grin on his face, he nodded. "My granddaddy made a couple of big strikes in the thirties and started the company. We became a subsidiary of Texaco a few years ago, but basically, we're still family run."

Her arms dropped and her eyes widened. "You're serious. You really are in oil?"

He grinned. "Isn't every Texan?"

It was her turn to grin. "No, I thought they were all cowboys."

His grin widened. "My mother's family owns the ranch."

She rolled her eyes.

"Really. I built a house on part of it and help work the cows."

Her eyes narrowed again.

He held up three fingers like a good boy scout. "Really. I'm serious."

"Then what are you doing substitute teaching?"

He shrugged. He couldn't very well tell her it was because he wanted to get to know his daughter. But he could tell her part of the truth, at least. "I always thought I'd like to teach. An acquaintance told me about this position and I thought it would give me a chance to find out if I wanted to herd kids or keep herding cows."

"And what did you decide?"

He rubbed the back of his neck. "As much as I love kids and as much as I enjoyed the last three weeks, I think herding cows and shuffling papers is a lot easier. And a lot more to my liking."

"The kids sure liked having you."

"I enjoyed being with them, too. But I've always liked setting my own schedule, being my own boss, taking a day or a week off when I want to. You can't do that teaching school."

"But you can in the oil business?"

"Two of my brothers, as well as my father, and one of my sisters are in the business. Well, one brother is gone more than he's there, but the other brother is always on the job and loves it. I help out with papers and business trips, but I spend a lot more time out at the ranch."

"I've heard that ranching is hard work."

"It is. But we have good managers on the job. I do a lot of paper shuffling out there, too. I actually climb onto the back of a cowpony about once or twice a week. And that's more because I want to, than because I have to. Ranching's changed a lot in the last twenty years."

"So, you'll be going back to Austin." It was a statement. He could almost hear the good-bye in her words.

"Austin's only an hour away."

She just nodded, looking straight ahead, and he knew what she was thinking. *Just an hour, but a different city, a long distance phone call away, busy lives, jobs, and things will just drift apart.* But he wasn't about to let them drift apart. He wanted Carly in his life. And he wanted Katie. But he had to be sure he wanted Katie for the right reasons, not just because she was Carly's mother.

"I'm not moving back right away. There's still something here in San Antonio I want to do."

"Oh?"

"Yeah." He reached over and crooked a hand around the back of her neck, his thumb massaging her nape. "Get to know you."

They talked about their college experiences over egg rolls and fried wontons, about childhood over egg drop soup, and about their dreams over sweet and sour shrimp and fried rice. By the time dinner was over, Adrian was amazed at how much you could learn about a person when you weren't being distracted by a child.

And everything he had learned about Katie made him like her more. She was smart, sweet, compassionate, a wonderful listener, and she had a great sense of humor.

By the time he was escorting her to her door, Adrian thought that even without her luscious body, Katie would be quite a catch. But did he really want to marry her? If Carly was out of the picture would he still be thinking about marrying Katie? Or was Carly the real reason he was considering it? And what about having more kids? Wouldn't he have to give that up?

Well, he didn't have to decide right now whether or not to marry Katie Simmons. Right now all he wanted was to get to know his daughter and decide what to do about her. Right now all he needed to do was be nice to Katie. He would just take things easy, just be a friend. Nothing more for now.

"Would you like to come in for dessert?" Most of Katie's face was in shadow, but moonlight spilled across her chin, her neck, the soft mounds of her breasts rising above her blue scoop neck blouse. The keys in her hand jingled faintly like erotic temple bells.

Adrian had to clear his throat before he could speak clearly. Just what did she have in mind? "Got another carrot cake in there?"

Her laughter, light and soft, floated to him. "No. Rum cake this time."

"Rum." Adrian could not take his eyes from her breasts. He remembered them in that rum-soaked shirt the first time he had come to this house, the material clinging to her skin.

She turned to open the door, pushing it wide. Reaching inside to flip on the light, golden light haloed her hair. She turned back with a questioning look and he could only nod and follow her inside, watching the sway of her hips, the swish of her skirt as she led him to the kitchen.

Katie dropped her keys into her purse, set it on the table and went to the sink to wash her hands. "Do you want coffee?"

He watched her dry her hands on a towel as she waited for his answer.

"Sure."

She nodded and turned to a cabinet. "I'll get the coffee going. You can get the mugs and plates. There. In that last cupboard."

Adrian opened the door she indicated and was greeted by at least twenty mugs, all different. He picked out one with pink flowers on it for Katie then reached to the back to pull out a Cincinnati Reds one for himself. His hand jostled a box and he just managed to catch it. A box of hypodermic syringes.

He stood looking down at it in surprise, then turned to find Katie looking at what he held, her eyes wide. Well, here it was, that "smoking gun" he had thought about last Sunday. The one he had promised himself to ask about before he jumped to conclusions. But all he could think was drug addict. He took a deep breath, trying to force his mind to quit racing and to think of a reason other than drugs for Katie to have a box of needles in her kitchen cabinet. His mind leapt to the only other possibility he could come up with. "Are you diabetic?"

The corner of her mouth quivered and he thought she was going to cry. But the quiver turned into a giggle. She pulled a cake container toward her and took off the lid. With one hand she waved toward the cake. "No, you've just discovered the secret to my greatly demanded rum cake."

"Rum cake?" He looked from Katie to the needles and back again, his mind in a swirl trying to follow the thread from drugs to diabetes to rum cake.

"You have to promise not to tell," she said reaching into a drawer and pulling out a cake knife.

"Not to tell what?"

"I use a needle to inject rum sauce into the cake. That way, even the center is rum soaked. My customers love it."

"Customers?"

"I do baking for people when they have parties and want homemade desserts and bread but don't want to make them themselves. And I supply a couple of restaurants with some desserts."

She turned and began cutting the cake, two pieces juicy with rum. She looked so normal and natural that it seemed crazy that just moments ago he had had suspicions that she was a drug user. Suspicions he had not voiced. Suspicions he had not let bloom into blatant distrust. Suspicions about her that had once again been allayed.

He set down the box of needles feeling almost triumphant. She had been indicted, judged, and acquitted. But he was the one who suddenly felt free. Laughing with the sudden joy of it he reached around her, took the cake knife from her hand, set it down, turned her, and kissed her full on the mouth.

Chapter Eight

KATIE WAS STUNNED BY THE FIERCE POSSESSIVENESS OF Adrian's kiss. It was as if he had been dancing around her ever since they had met, but had at last swooped in to claim her as his, finally and forever. And now that she knew something about him she was ready to let him in. She let herself flow into that possession, welcoming it, opening opening her mouth when his tongue slid along the seam of her lips.

She slid her hands from his chest around his leanly fleshed ribs and across his back. Beneath the soft cotton of his shirt she could feel the muscles she had admired that day in the pool, except that his mouth was distracting her. There was just too much sensation to revel in, tongue now lightly touching lips, now plunging deep, again playful. His hands moved from her upper arms across her back, and down the length of the muscles along each side of her spine to the small of her waist. They only paused there a moment before sliding over the curve of her rump to pull her hips forward into a more intimate contact with his.

She felt him against the length of her, thighs touching thighs, muscled abdomen touching belly, chest pressed to breasts, and all of him, including that part pressed to her groin, was hard and urgent.

How could he be so hard when she was turning to liquid? Desire was melting her insides and she could feel it pooling in her panties. If they didn't stop this instant it would be running down her legs.

His tongue raked the inside of her mouth and when she returned the gesture she felt his response. Her hips shifted, almost of their own accord, to settle her more snugly against that response. Good Lord, it had been so long since she had experienced this. She had forgotten just how powerful a thing desire was. They really should stop now before things got out of hand.

She could feel the flex of his back muscles as he held her to him, felt the strength of his hands spread over her buttocks, warm and digging in. Her own hands seemed to have a mind of their own, following the ridges of his muscles downward to splay over his buns. They felt so good, so tight and hard and that sensation went straight up to her brain and bounced to nipples and groin.

More goo. She was positively flooding. This had to stop.

His right hand left her buttock and she knew instinctively where it was headed. She wanted it there, she knew how it would feel, and her breast grew taut with anticipation.

His fingers skimmed along the side curve of her breast. Oh God. She thought she had remembered how good it felt to have a man touch her there. But she had forgotten how that simple sensation could travel throughout the body to bring every cell to red alert and pulsing with a demand for more.

She couldn't let this go on. There was only one logical conclusion to what they were doing and she didn't think she was ready to take that step with Adrian.

She shifted slightly to give him access to more of her breast. He was quick to take advantage of the chance to conquer more territory. At first the peak eluded him, but with a further shifting she managed to place it full into his hand.

She felt his warmth seep into her and when his finger and thumb came together to gently tweak, she was ready to climax right then and there. She was open and throbbing and needing to be filled. And he had all the proper equipment to do the filling.

She didn't think she could stop this now and wasn't sure she wanted to. She felt like she was on a freight train headed downhill with no brakes.

That's when the phone rang. Katie's eyes flew open, and the freight train screeched to a halt. Adrian had lifted his head but was looking at her with pleading in his eyes, hoping she would ignore the phone.

"It's almost midnight," she said. "There could be a problem with Carly."

She could see the frustration knotting his forehead, heard the small groan of protest he made. But he nodded in agreement and reached back to pick up the phone, handed it to her, and turned to lean back against the sink, arms folded.

"Hello."

"Katie, I'm sorry to call this late," Katie recognized Miriam Kisor's voice, "but Carly's not feeling well."

"What's wrong?" As soon as she said the words, the frustration vanished from Adrian's face and he stood up straight, stepping nearer and hovering over her.

"She said she didn't feel well earlier. 'Achy and icky' is what she said. But now she's developing a bit of a fever and wants her mommy, so I thought I'd better call."

"I'm glad you did. I'll be right over to get her. Thanks, Miriam."

"I'll keep her here if you want," Miriam said. "It's probably just one of those twenty-four hour things, but I thought I should call."

"I appreciate it, but I'd better come and get her."

The receiver wasn't even on the hook before Adrian was demanding, "Is it Carly? Is she all right?"

"She has a fever. I'm going to walk down to Miriam's and bring her home." She placed her hand on Adrian's chest, caressing, a non-verbal promise to continue where they left off another time. "Thanks for a wonderful evening..."

His hand came up to cover hers, squeezing in silent acceptance of her promise. "I'm coming with you."

Katie opened her mouth to protest. There was no need for Adrian to go to the Kisor's with her. She had been handling this kind of thing alone for nearly three years now. But she could see the concern in his eyes and suddenly she realized just how much she had missed having another set of shoulders to help carry the responsibility.

"I'd like that," she said.

They walked together the two doors down to the Kisor's with Adrian's arm comfortingly around her shoulders. Miriam was waiting at the door for them. Her brows lifted in question when she saw Adrian but she didn't say anything, just opened the door wider.

When Adrian stepped inside the Kisor's home he saw Carly snugged up on one end of the couch clutching Stripey Tiger and looking miserable. Angela was curled into a ball on the other end sound asleep. Carly's eyes looked red and bleary and her face was pale, and he wanted to snatch her up into his arms and rush her immediately to the emergency room.

Carly held up her arms to Katie. "Mommy!"

"Hi, Sweetie. How are you feeling?" Katie leaned down for Carly's hug and kissed her daughter lightly on the forehead.

"I hurt all over. Hi, Mr. Wright."

Adrian wanted to rush over for a hug, too, but knew he was

here on sufferance only and managed to contain himself to a mere, "Hello, Carly," and a touch to her forehead, brushing back her hair. He knew he was worried and inexperienced in these things, but, to him, it seemed like she was burning up.

"You'll be all right." Katie straightened and turned to Miriam. "I hope Angela doesn't get it."

You'll be all right? How could she so blithely dismiss this fever, Adrian wondered. Why wasn't she taking her temperature?

Miriam shrugged and gave a quick laugh. "Can't be helped now, I guess. But I hope Carly feels better soon." She glanced at Adrian then back at Katie. "You two have a good time?"

Katie smiled and Adrian saw that tell-tale flush of hers start to flow down her neck. "Very nice."

Miriam arched a brow at Katie. "Sorry I had to interrupt. That's the way it goes with kids, though."

Adrian danced back and forth from one foot to the other. How could the two of them be so calm, talking about how their evening went when Carly was lying there possibly at death's door? Shouldn't they be doing something? Calling the doctor? Giving her...giving her...well, something? He felt so out of his depth and needed to do something. Anything.

Katie brushed Carly's hair back. "Do you think you can walk home, Sweetheart, or should I carry you?"

Adrian stepped forward, reaching for Carly. At last, not only something physical he could do, but a chance to cuddle his daughter and comfort her. "I'll carry her."

Katie looked at him as if she would protest, but then she smiled and nodded her thanks.

Adrian handed Stripey Tiger to Katie and Carly's sweet little arms went around his neck as he picked her up. She laid her head on his shoulder and he bent his head to press his cheek to hers, feeling the heat of her fever. It frightened him to think of her small body attacked by something he had no power to protect her from, no matter how tightly he held her.

Miriam opened the door for them. "Give me a call in the morning. Let me know how she is."

"I will," Katie said. "Thanks."

When Adrian carried Carly inside her house, Katie directed him down the hallway to the bedrooms. Carly lifted her head and yawned. "Can I sleep with you, Mommy?"

"Sure, Sweetheart."

Katie led Adrian into the master bedroom and turned back the covers on the bed. Adrian took just a moment to hold Carly tight against him and place a very fatherly kiss on her forehead, closing his eyes at the sheer wonder of it. It was the first time he had ever gotten to tuck her into bed, and he wanted to savor every second of it, even if the circumstances weren't the best.

He laid her down on the bed and pulled the covers up.

Katie was coming out of the bathroom shaking a thermometer and Adrian sighed with relief. "I'm sure that fever isn't much over a hundred," Katie said, "but I thought I'd better check to make sure." She smiled down at Carly and stuck the thermometer under her tongue.

Not much over a hundred? How could she tell?

It seemed like at least two hours passed before Katie pulled the thermometer back out and looked at it.

"What is it, Mommy?"

"Not too bad, Sweetie. One hundred point two. You go to sleep now. I'll be in in a few minutes." Katie tucked Stripey Tiger in beside her and Carly turned on her side putting one arm around her stuffed toy.

She was asleep almost instantly, and Adrian thought he had never seen such an angelic sight. He wanted nothing more than to stand there the rest of the night watching her sleep, guarding her to make sure she was all right. But Katie tugged at his sleeve and, reluctantly, he turned to follow her back down the hall to the living room shaking his head in amazement.

"How did you know what her temperature was before you took it with the thermometer?"

Katie laughed and pointed to her lips. "The Mommy Thermometer. When I kissed her, I knew. Most accurate fever detector made."

"I was so worried about her."

"I know. Thanks for your help, Adrian. You never did get that piece of cake, did you? Would you like to take it along?"

She was dismissing him and he didn't want to go. What if something happened in the night? What if Carly's temperature suddenly shot up? She was his daughter, damn it, and he was being evicted from the premises.

She paused beside the front door and he drew her into his arms, holding her lightly and looking down at her. "Would you like me to stay the night? I could sleep on the couch."

She shook her head, but it seemed that her look was more than a little wistful, as if she wished she had a good enough reason to say yes. "We'll be fine."

"Are you going to call a doctor?"

"I'll see how she is in the morning."

He nodded, wondering how early he could reasonably show up here tomorrow. "See you about noon?"

She smiled and nodded. "I'll make us some lunch."

He kissed her then, lightly, wanting more but knowing it was the wrong time. "See you both tomorrow."

By eleven thirty the next morning, Adrian was pacing the floor, which wasn't easy considering the size of his apartment. He had already been out once this morning to get something for Carly and just happened to drive by their house on the way home. He hadn't seen anyone, hadn't seen any sign that they were even up. It hadn't been easy to drive on by.

But it was now eleven thirty. He had set that as the time he could leave, drive slow, and get there, well, maybe just a bit too early, but surely they'd be up. He had wanted to call, but been afraid of waking Carly. But now he could go.

He picked up Carly's present and left, admonishing himself to drive slowly. He told himself it wasn't so bad when he just missed the left turn light and had to wait. It would mean that he would get there closer to noon.

He tried to reason that the elderly gentleman who slowed suddenly ahead of him and took an eternity to turn left was put there by God to keep him from showing up too soon. Even the dog that ran across the street in front of him, making him throw on the brakes was just helping him not to show up unreasonably early.

Those things also made him realize how much better it would have been if he could have just stayed there last night. And every night. And not just so he could be there when Carly was sick. He wanted to go to bed with Katie. And not just to sleep. Damn, she felt good in his arms. She might appear all cool and calm on the outside with her ice blue eyes and cool silver hair and sweet smile, but she had turned to fire as soon as he had touched her.

Finally, he pulled into their driveway. It was ten till twelve. Not bad.

As soon as Katie opened the door, Adrian saw Carly sitting on the couch with a blanket over her, alive and apparently much better, smiling and waving at him. Adrian took the first relaxed breath he had taken since the night before.

All kinds of good baking smells greeted Adrian—cake, bread, something with apples. It was a lot better than any perfume he had ever smelled and it was all wafting around Katie. He thought he would forever after associate the smell of baking bread with this woman. He couldn't help but kiss her before he asked, "How's Carly?"

"Her fever is gone but I thought she should stay quiet for the rest of the day," Katie said.

Adrian sat beside Carly on the couch and handed her the game he had bought. "I brought you something to do," he said.

"A new *Chutes and Ladders!* Thanks, Mr. Wright." She opened the box and took out the board. "Will you play with me?"

"Sure. I thought I might be able to win with a new game board. Your old one just didn't seem to like me. I'm challenging you to a game right now."

Carly slid off the couch and spread the game on the floor. "Can I go first?"

Adrian grinned up at Katie before joining Carly on the floor. "Want to play?"

"I'll just finish lunch. Maybe you can beat Carly at that game. I've never been able to."

"So! I'm facing an expert at *Chutes and Ladders*, eh?"

"Yep. I always win." Carly grinned while she flicked the spinner. She got a two, just missing the ladder up. "Well, almost always."

Adrian spun and with a four landed on a space with a ladder, enabling him to climb up. He gave an evil chuckle and pushed the spinner toward her.

With a determined look, Carly spun, got another two and with a triumphant, "Hah!" landed in the same space as Adrian.

"Oh no!" Adrian exaggerated a moan when he landed on a space with a chute, sliding downward.

"Sounds like you're going down in defeat," Katie called from the kitchen.

"The game isn't over yet!" Adrian answered.

But it soon was over with Carly the smiling winner, and Katie called them in for lunch.

"You were right," Adrian said to Katie as he helped Carly into a chair. "She's hard to beat. But I'm going to do it. Right after lunch."

"Good luck."

Lunch was sandwiches on homemade bread with barley and bean soup. And there was the interrupted rum cake from the night before for dessert. It was a wonderful meal and Adrian told Katie so more than once.

Adrian noticed that Carly's appetite was a bit off, but he more than made up for her lack. Carly got up with her plate in hand and headed for the kitchen.

"Just put it there on the counter and go rest, Carly. When you're sick you don't have to help."

"Thanks, Mommy. Will you play another game now, Mr. Wright?"

Adrian gathered his plate and silverware. "Just as soon as I help with the dishes. I'm not sick."

When he went into the kitchen, Adrian saw what he had been smelling. There were two cakes, three pies, rolls, and four loaves of bread.

"Looks like you're getting ready for a party." Adrian rinsed his plate and put it into the dishwasher.

"I am. Not mine, though. I'm baking for a friend who's having a dinner party tonight."

Adrian looked over the pies with crust that looked so flaky it was ready to crumble. "Lucky friend."

Katie laughed. "I have to take this stuff over to her in a few minutes. Would you mind staying here with Carly? I can take her, but I'd really rather she stay here and rest."

Adrian clutched the edge of the sink to keep his hands from

shaking. Katie didn't realize what she was offering him. To have his daughter all to himself for even a brief time, to be entrusted with her care, to just have some time to sit and play games with her, was priceless.

He tried to sound casual, off hand, when he turned to her and responded. "Sure. I'm going to beat her at *Chutes and Ladders* if it takes all afternoon."

"Great. Thanks. I'll just get this stuff boxed up and I'll go. I won't be long. An hour or less."

"Take all the time you need. Getting to know you two was all I had on my agenda for today anyway, remember?"

"I remember." She leaned into him, and his arm automatically went around her to caress her back. She lifted herself on tiptoe to kiss him, but before he could take advantage of her kiss and deepen it, she had moved away. "Just a reminder," she said, mischievously.

"I don't need reminders, but I'll take whatever I can get." He bent for another kiss and this one was more than a mere reminder. He wondered if her "Mommy Thermometer" could detect the fever in him. When she pulled away and took a deep calming breath, he was surprised that the heat of that kiss had not scorched the boxes sitting on the counter, melted the frosting on the cakes, and charred the rolls.

Her voice was shaky when she answered. "No, you don't need reminders. But I might need one to remind me to stop."

He hugged her tighter. "I don't give those kind of reminders."

"Mr. Wright, are you going to play another game?"

They laughed as they said in unison, "But Carly does."

"I'll be right there, Carly," Adrian answered.

Katie began putting the baked goods into boxes. "Speaking of parties," Adrian said, "my father is celebrating his sixtieth birthday on Saturday and the family is having a big party. Will you and Carly come with me, meet the clan?"

Katie turned to look up at him solemnly. He could tell what she was thinking. The same thing he had realized the moment the invitation was out of his mouth. That their relationship was about to change again. That it was about to take a serious turn. That he wanted to take her home to meet his parents. If she said yes, then she was essentially saying that she was as serious about their relationship as he was, and he didn't realize he was holding his breath until she answered.

"I'd love to go with you. But are you sure it will be all right?"

He almost laughed with happiness at her response. "If it's a typical family gathering, one or two more won't make any difference. But I'll give Mom a call to let her know."

"So, there'll be a lot of people there?"

"A hundred or so. Carly will have lots of things to keep her entertained. There's usually a lot of kids and there's a pool, swing set, games."

"Can I bring anything? Bake a cake or pie or something?"

He kissed her lightly on the nose. "First time you come, you're company. After that, you're family. Then you can bring something."

She laughed. "Okay. So we'll be company. I'll let you wait on me hand and foot."

He gave a mock salaam. "Your wish is my command."

She handed him a box of pies. "To the back seat of the car, Slave!"

As soon as Katie left, Adrian sat down on the floor to play another game of *Chutes and Ladders* with Carly. She won.

After going down in defeat a third time Adrian leaned back against the couch, threw up his hands, and said, "I give up. You're the champ."

Carly gave him a concerned look. "Would you like me to let you win a game?"

Adrian felt a glow at the sweetness of her concern for his feelings. He grinned at her. "No, I would not. I will beat you one of these days all on my own."

"What would you like to do now? Mommy should be home soon. It usually doesn't take her long to take stuff when she bakes for people."

"Oh? Does she bake for people a lot?"

"All the time. She bakes to get money. The last time she baked for a big party, she got a lot of money and she bought me a new dress."

Adrian sat up with a start. Katie was baking to get money to buy Carly clothes? He had grown up with money. Had always had it. He had never given it a thought that Katie and Carly might not be in good financial shape. He looked around the newly refurbished living room. It didn't seem like they needed money that badly. But how was he to know? Katie was widowed and a stay-at-home mom. Maybe their finances weren't so good after all. It was something he would have to check out. In the meantime, he had a daughter to entertain.

"What would you like to do, Carly?"

Carly looked up at him hopefully. "We could watch *The Little Mermaid*."

"Didn't you watch that not long ago?"

She shrugged. "It's my favorite!"

"Okay." He put the video in and sat on the couch with Carly snuggled up against his side and his arm around her. He couldn't have thought of a better way to spend a Saturday afternoon.

Chapter Nine

I T'S A CIRCUS!" CARLY TUGGED HER HAND FREE OF KATIE'S TO point. "Look! Ponies!"

Adrian shook his head. The transformation that took place in the back yard of his parents' house every year for his father's birthday never ceased to amaze him. It was strung with lights and streamers and the combination tennis/basketball court had been turned into a dance floor with a five piece band getting set up on one corner of it. Later there would be Indian dancing, too. Tables and chairs were scattered around the yard and there were several tables full of food lined up on the patio. There was a game of horseshoes going on in the back by a shed and a game of volleyball was getting started. The two ponies Carly had spotted were tied to a fence and swishing their tails.

"It does look like a circus," Katie agreed.

Adrian snorted but he was grinning. "More like a zoo."

"Can I pet the ponies? Please?" Carly clutched his hand with both of hers and looked up at him with pleading eyes. She was so excited she was jumping up and down.

"How about a ride instead?" Adrian asked her.

Adrian thought Carly's eyes would bulge out of her head. She turned to her mother. "Can I?"

Katie looked at him a little uncertainly. "She's never ridden by herself before."

He gave her a reassuring nod. "I'll take care of her." They headed toward the ponies with Carly skipping eagerly between them. "Besides, Mack and Zeke are two of the gentlest ponies I've ever seen. We bring them up from the ranch every year for the younger kids to ride."

"Adrian! It's about time you got here!" Jace clapped him on the back and Adrian noticed Carly's shoulders slump. He could just hear what she was thinking, *Oh no. Adults have to talk and talk and I'll never get to those ponies.* But she smiled politely, even if she did keep eyeing the ponies and bouncing impatiently.

Adrian introduced everyone.

"Adrian's told me about you," he said. "But not much."

"He hasn't told me much about his family, either," Katie answered.

"Hmm. Him big, strong, silent Indian type," Jace mocked. "Just ask me what you want to know. I'll fill you in, tell you all the rotten things he did to me when we were kids, how he skipped school, blamed me for that big fire that burned down the barn—"

"You are the one who burned down the barn."

Jace rubbed the back of his neck. "Well, you were there, too."

"I was the cowboy. You were the Indian who had to use real flaming arrows."

Jace grinned. "I couldn't think of any other way to get you off the barn roof."

"Sounds like your parents had their hands full with you two," Katie said.

"These two? Finest sons a man could have." A tall, lanky man who could only be described as a Texas cowboy leaned into the circle between the two brothers with a hand on each of their shoulders. He was blond and fair and blue-eyed, and only in build did he resemble his sons.

"Dad, this is Katie Simmons and her daughter Carly," Adrian said. "Katie, my father, Houston Wright."

"Happy birthday, Mr. Wright." Katie held out the gift she had brought and Adrian's father tucked it under one arm, took her hand in his big, warm one, and leaned down to kiss her cheek.

"Why, thank you kindly. But call me Houston, Honey. Everybody calls me Houston." He shook hands with Carly. "You too, Becky. You call me Houston, too."

Carly giggled. "My name's Carly."

Houston leaned down as if to tell Carly a secret. "I call all the little girls Becky. That way, I never get the names wrong."

"Isn't Houston a place?" Carly asked.

"Yep. And one of the heroes of Texas independence. All my brothers are named for the heroes of the Alamo. There's Austin and Travis and Bowie and Crockett and me."

"I'm just glad you didn't continue the family tradition," Jace said wryly.

"Only because your ma wouldn't let me!" He chuckled. "But seems to me there's a certain young lady here who is gettin' fed up with all this nonsense and keeps eyein' them ponies over there. Ain't it about time to give this kid a ride?"

"We were just heading over that way," Adrian said.

"Well, git on with it, Son. We'll be eatin' pretty soon and then I'm goin' to need some help openin' all them presents. Maybe Becky'll sit next to me and give me a hand."

Carly grinned. "Okay! I like opening presents."

Houston gave her a wink and walked on to greet other guests who were just arriving.

"Can I ride the pony now?" Carly asked, obviously trying not to sound too impatient.

"Right this minute," Adrian answered, snatching a couple of

apples from a fruit laden table on the way to the ponies. He greeted each pony with a hand to its nose and then ran his hand over their necks and checked the saddle cinches. He handed an apple to Carly. "This is Mack," he told her, slapping a black and white pinto on the neck. Give him that apple and he'll be your friend for life."

Mack was already reaching for the apple and Carly drew back. Adrian bent down to enfold her against him so that she faced the pony. "Just hold it out with your hand flat and straight. He might slobber on you a bit, but he won't bite. He's more interested in apples than fingers."

Carly did as he said and the pony made short work of the apple, then looked for another.

"Greedy little beast, isn't he?" He gave her the other apple. "Give this one to Zeke or he'll be jealous."

Carly held out the other apple to the second pony, which was black except for a white z shaped streak down his shoulder.

"Which one do you want to ride first?"

Carly looked from one to the other and then chose Zeke. Adrian told her how to mount and then had to give her a boost, settling her feet into the stirrups. He handed her the reins, and while Jace and Katie stood looking on, Adrian led the pony around the house and down the street holding onto the bridle.

He was so proud of her. He wanted to shout out to the whole street, to the whole world that this was his daughter. He settled for grinning himself silly.

"Think you can handle him all by yourself, now?" He asked her. She looked uncertain a moment, but nodded. He let go of the bridle and turned away. Just as he knew it would, the little pony followed closely behind him, nudging him with its nose every few steps.

When they came back into the yard Katie looked at them with surprise but smiled proudly, and Adrian knew in that moment that she felt just as proud of Carly as he did. And he knew that Carly was just as much Katie's child as she was his. Maybe more so. He had no more right to this child than the woman who had raised her.

When they came to a halt, Carly leaned forward to give Zeke a hug. "Thank you, Zeke. I love you."

"Would you like Zeke to be your pony?"

Carly's eyes widened. "Really? Can I take him home with me? Mom?" She turned to Katie for permission to take the pony home.

Adrian laughed and pulled Carly from Zeke's back. "I think Zeke will be a lot happier at the ranch, Carly. But whenever you come to visit, Zeke is yours and I'll teach you how to take care of him. But right now, I think there are a few other kids who want a ride."

Jace was helping one of the other kids onto Mack and several others were waiting for turns, now that they saw the ponies in action.

Carly patted Zeke one more time before Adrian helped another little girl into the saddle and turned the pony over to a cowhand from the ranch who had come with the ponies to help out.

"Bye, Zeke." Carly waved as the pony was led away. She turned to Adrian. "Can I visit him soon?"

"And often, I hope," Adrian answered, giving her hand a squeeze and looking at Katie.

"I hope so, too." Katie was looking right into his eyes. Right then Adrian knew that the three of them belonged together and that she knew it, too. It was just a matter of formalities. All he had to do was ask her.

Someone began ringing the dinner bell and they headed up toward the patio, Adrian's arm slung around Katie's shoulder.

Katie leaned into Adrian, reveling in the feel of his lean hardness, his easy stride, the heavy weight of his arm draped across her, casual, and just where it seemed to belong. It felt good. It felt right.

"Adrian! Where have you been hiding, brother?" Adrian exchanged a couple of backslaps with a dark-skinned Indian man, with long hair and a choker made of silver and turquoise.

"Joe! Good to see you. I want you to meet Katie and her daughter, Carly."

Joe took Katie's hand and squeezed it between his, nodding solemnly. "I been eyeing her since you got here. I was hoping she was up for grabs." He eyed the possessive way Adrian's arm tightened. "But I guess not." He bent to greet Carly with a squeeze to her hand, too. Then he caught two passing women and introduced them as his sisters, Angela and Marie.

After a few more introductions, Katie was shaking her head in confusion. "I didn't know you had so many brothers and sisters, Adrian."

Adrian looked surprised for a moment, then shrugged. "Well most of the people you've just met are actually my cousins." He looked around at some of the people they had greeted. "Jace is my brother and so is Luke. Vickie is my sister. The rest were cousins. To an Indian, it doesn't really matter a whole lot. Cousin or brother is just about the same thing."

"I think I like the concept," Katie said, smiling, thinking of her own scant and scattered family. "It makes you all seem so much..."

"Closer?"

She nodded wistfully. "Yes. It's comforting."

"Wait until you meet my grandparents." He indicated an older couple sitting on the patio surrounded by several children. The woman was definitely Indian with nearly white hair that laid across her shoulders in long, thick braids, and eyes blacker than Adrian's.

She wore a long denim skirt and a bright fringed shawl lay draped over the back of her chair. The hand she reached up to greet them with was filled with silver and turquoise rings, and heavy bracelets dangled from her wrists.

"Adrian, my son," she said warmly, as Adrian bent to kiss her cheek.

"Grandma Julie," he murmured. He nodded to the man sitting next to her, "Grandpa Matt. This is Katie Simmons and her daughter, Carly. Katie, Carly, this is my grandmother, Julie and my grandfather Matt Madison."

Adrian's grandfather nodded, but his arm did not leave his wife's. Katie could tell they were still very much in love.

"So, this is the woman who has taken you away from us so much lately," his grandmother said. Although her words were slightly accented, there was nothing unfriendly about them, and she tightly squeezed Katie's hand then drew Carly close to her as if to claim her as her own.

Carly did not seem at all reluctant to be drawn in. A loving grandmother was something else Carly had missed out on.

Adrian's grandmother gently caressed Carly's cheek and fingered her long, dark braids. "Is she one of the People?"

Katie looked questioningly to Adrian, not understanding exactly what his grandmother wanted to know. Adrian looked more uneasy than she had ever seen him and she wondered why. "She wants to know if Carly is Indian."

"Ah!" Katie said, understanding dawning. Then to Grandma Julie she said, "I have often wondered the same thing. But since Carly is adopted, I don't know if she is part Indian or not."

Grandma Julie nodded. "Then let us assume that she is." She put her arm around Carly and hugged her tightly as if the matter were settled.

"I'm an Indian?" Carly asked, eyes wide and hopeful.

Katie wasn't sure what to tell Carly, but before she could speak, Adrian said, "You are now." And that seemed to answer Carly's question to her satisfaction.

"Are you ready to eat, Carly?" Grandma Julie asked.

Carly squirmed and looked pleadingly up at Katie. "Yes, but..."

Grandma Julie leaned close to Carly. "But you need a bathroom first?"

Carly nodded in relief.

"I'll take her." Grandma Julie stood and Carly seemed quite happy to go with the understanding woman.

Adrian's mother was a younger version of Grandma Julie, complete with long braids that were dark instead of white, and a lot of silver and turquoise jewelry. Katie liked her immediately.

Katie saw Grandma Julie come back outside with Carly and help her get some food. Then the two of them sat down together. Carly looked around for her mother, but when she found Katie, she just waved and turned back to Grandma Julie, content to be with her and not giving Katie any kind of look that said, Come and rescue me.

Katie and Adrian went along the tables filling their own plates. There seemed to be some of everything from beef and fried chicken to venison and other wild game, and of course, Indian fried bread.

They sat with Jace and Joe, and those two filled Katie in on some more of their juvenile antics.

When a cake blazing with candles was brought out everyone gathered around Houston to sing Happy Birthday and get a piece. Then he sat on a chair to open presents. He motioned to Carly. "Come on over here, Darlin'. Didn't you promise to help open these presents?"

Another child was appointed to bring presents one at a time.

Houston opened a couple with Carly's enthusiastic help then stopped her on the third one. "Wait a minute here, Becky. This here present ain't for me. I think that name tag says Mattie on it." He looked around for his wife and handed her the present he had bought for her.

She laughed and bent to kiss the top of his head before opening the gift. She took out a gold bracelet and kissed him again to the applause of the crowd.

Houston took the next present and peered intently at the tag. "Well, by gum, this ain't my present, either. Can you read what that says there, Becky?"

Carly looked at the tag and her eyes opened wide in surprise. "It says Carly Simmons! That's me!"

"Well, then, I guess you'll have to open that one all by yourself."

Carly tore into the present. It was a Barbie doll. And as she hugged Houston and thanked him, he caught Adrian's eye and winked at him.

After that, there were presents for everyone. Katie was given a silver necklace which Adrian helped her put on. "I didn't expect to come to a birthday party and get a present," she said.

Adrian laughed. "He does this every year. He says it's his way of thanking the Good Lord for another fine year with family around him."

Katie fingered her necklace and looked around at the kids happily playing with their new toys. "You have a very special family, Adrian."

Adrian could hear a wistfulness in her voice as if she were longing to be a part of it. He squeezed her hand. He wanted to ask her right then to become a part of it by marrying him, but it wasn't the time or place. But it had to be soon. It was getting harder and harder to leave her and Carly every night. He wanted to spend more and more time with them, and the only way that was possible was to spend their nights together. And that's what he wanted to do. And he was pretty sure Katie wanted that just as much as he did.

Someone started some games and the first one was just for mother-daughter teams. Carly dragged Katie out to the lawn to participate and Adrian leaned back in his chair to watch.

"Seems you've changed your mind about Mrs. Simmons."

Adrian cocked a glance at his brother, Jace, sitting there with a smug look on his face.

"Yeah. I've changed my mind about Mrs. Simmons." Adrian buried his face in his drink to avoid adding, *you were right.*

Jace laughed. "I can see why."

Adrian put down his drink and swung around to face his brother. "It's a lot more than that, Jace. She's sweet and good, a wonderful mother." He stopped to laugh at himself and run a hand over his belly. "And if she keeps feeding me like she has the last couple of weeks, I'm going to have to join an exercise club. You should taste her homemade bread and cakes and pies."

Jace leaned back in his chair, folded his arms, shook his head and laughed again. "When you change your mind, you really change your mind. There's no in between for you, is there?"

Adrian grinned, feeling more than a little abashed. He knew what a pig-headed ass he could be at times. "When I'm wrong, I admit it."

"You were certainly right about Carly, though. She's a terrific kid."

"Yeah." Adrian felt the same happiness bubble up inside him whenever he thought about his daughter. "Did you see how she rode old Zeke? She's a natural. I'll have her herding cows and roping calves in no time."

A troubled frown creased Jace's brows. "You're not still thinking about taking her away from her mother, are you?"

"Nope. I do want Carly and I'm going to have her one way or another." Adrian leaned forward intently. "But I want it all. I want Katie. I want us to be a family. I'm going to marry her, Jace. I decided today to ask her. The idea has been nibbling at me for a while, but today, seeing her here, well, she belongs. She belongs with me and with this family. And so does Carly."

"You haven't told her yet, have you?" Jace was looking at him seriously, all traces of laughter gone.

A tiny thread of apprehension began to tangle itself into a knot in Adrian's stomach. He leaned forward with his elbows on the table and looked straight into his brother's eyes. "There's no reason I have to tell her anything," he growled.

Jace just lifted one brow. "Isn't there?"

Adrian waved away a fly that tried to land in his drink. "What difference would it make?"

"You tell me."

"She'd be glad." Even as he said it, Adrian knew he was grasping at straws. "She's told me about guys who only pretended to like Carly to get to her. She'd be glad to know that I have more than just a superficial interest in Carly."

"Would she?"

Adrian sat back feeling totally bleak as he faced the bare truth. "On the other hand she might be madder'n heck that for once a guy used her to get to Carly."

"And what about Carly?"

"Carly?"

"Some day you'll want her to know who you are. If you do marry Katie, could you tell Carly and keep something like this from your wife?"

Adrian didn't say anything. He couldn't. The pain inside was too great. But it was a pain he had created himself by not approaching Katie and Carly openly, right from the beginning.

But how could he have known then that his life would become so entangled with theirs?

"So, what are you going to do?"

"I don't want to lose her, Jace." Adrian could hear the desperation in his own voice.

"So, what are you going to do?"

"Damn!"

Chapter Ten

ALL THE WAY BACK FROM THE PARTY KATIE AND CARLY KEPT up a happy chatter. All the way back from the party Adrian drove with hell burning in his gut.

Carly asked what kind of stall her pony, Zeke, had. What did he eat? Was he good friends with the other ponies?

Adrian had given Carly one more ride on the stout little pony before they left. Carly had hugged and kissed Zeke good-bye and told him she was his new owner and would see him soon.

Katie talked about his mother's flowers and where in her own yard she was going to plant the cuttings of Asiatic jasmine and Mandeville vine she had been given.

All Adrian could think of was how wrong it all was. For one thing, they were headed in the wrong direction. He shouldn't be taking them back to San Antonio but to his house out at the ranch where Carly could pet Zeke and stuff him with carrots and apples. Katie could cook to her heart's content and he could work in the garden his mother had helped him plant but which needed a lot more care than he had given it lately. And later, after they had tucked Carly in for the night, he and Katie could...

But it wasn't going to happen. Not tonight. And not anytime soon, either, unless he could convince Katie to marry him next week. And what chance of that would there be once he told Katie who he really was?

The problem was, he just didn't know how Katie would react. Would she be thrilled to know that she and the natural father of her child had just happened to fall in love with each other? Well, why wouldn't she be? Wasn't that the best thing that could have happened? The best solution to who got custody of Carly? But, damn! Just because it was the best, most logical solution didn't mean it would set right with a woman.

Not that women weren't logical. They just seemed to have a logic all their own that just happened to run counter to any thinking a man did.

The hellfire in his gut was about to burn out of control and Adrian knew that very little of it could be attributed to his father's famous chili.

He wished he could just marry Katie and not have to tell her anything. He could do that. He was pretty sure she'd say yes. Then after a few weeks, or months, or years, he could casually mention that he was really Carly's father. Katie would laugh and snuggle up to him and say she had known it all along. Somehow women always seemed to know stuff before a man confessed it. Heck, they knew stuff even before the man knew there was something he needed to confess. So why didn't Katie know who he was?

Maybe she did. Maybe she had known right from the first but hadn't said anything and was just waiting for him to bring it up so she could throw herself into his arms, say it was all okay and she would marry him as soon as they could get a license.

No, that would be too easy. There was no way Katie could know or even suspect that he was Carly's father. To wait until after they were married to tell her was pure cowardice, not to mention potentially lethal to their relationship and their marriage. Starting a marriage with secrets and lies was not advisable.

Adrian glanced over at Katie's now smiling face wishing it could always be this way.

"Bite the bullet, Son," his father would say. And that's just what he would have to do. Adrian just hoped he didn't choke on it.

As soon as Katie opened the door for him the next evening, Adrian was enveloped in the smell of cinnamon and apples—and Katie's arms. Almost before the door was closed she was melting into him like butter. It was as if they were two halves of a whole reunited at last. They were.

He felt every inch of her pressed up against him. His cheek nestled against her hair and the fragrance of her mingled pleasantly with the baking smells from the kitchen.

Her arms locked around his ribs and his about her shoulders. He felt her thighs firm along his own. Her feet were bare and one foot was caressing his ankle.

Her head tilted back ready for his kiss and as he lowered his head to claim her, he thought this was the way it should be. Totally one. Totally wanting each other. Totally open with each other.

Yeah, right. Totally open. His hypocrisy nearly soured the kiss in his mouth. But Katie's sweetness overcame it and he sank into her love like a weary body into a down mattress.

The kiss was long and tantalizing. Too tantalizing. He knew right where he wanted it to lead, what the culmination of her greeting could be, but he also knew it was the most dishonest thing he could do right now. She had to know who he was before their relationship went any further. The problem was, when he told her, it might be the end of any relationship they might have.

At that thought, his gut twisted and he hugged her more fiercely to him, wanting desperately to bind her to him forever with the force of his embrace. If he had ruined everything by his deception, he would at least have this last sweet moment to cherish.

Their kiss came apart on a sigh and Katie's moan struck through his vitals like a sword.

"Is this what you wanted to discuss with me?" she asked. He could hear the humor in her tone and feel her lips move into a smile against his chest. "Is this why you said you wanted to be alone tonight?"

Yes! he wanted to cry. Yes! He rubbed the back of her neck and slipped his fingers into her hair, holding her head to him. He savored her nearness. He had to tell her. But first there was something even more important he had to say. "I love you, Katie."

He felt her grip him tighter. "I love you, too. I never thought I could love again, Adrian. You showed me how wrong I was."

Oh, God! This was going to be harder than he had imagined. To have her, only to possibly lose her! He had never realized until right this moment how incomplete he was. How much a part of his life she and Carly had become. If he lost them now, it would be like ripping out his guts. He wanted Katie in his life and in his bed. He wanted them to be together always. "I want you, Katie. I want to marry you. I want you and Carly and me to be a family."

She leaned back to look up at him. Her eyes were shining with love and acceptance. She started to answer but he shook his head in quick negation. Before she gave him an answer he had to finish what he had to say even if it meant forever killing the love light sparkling in her eyes.

"There's something I have tell you, Katie. Something you have to know before you give me an answer."

Katie tilted her head, suppressing a smile, as if she didn't believe that there was anything he could tell her that would change things. A merry twinkle played mischievously in her eyes. "You already have a wife and three kids?"

He gripped her arms and looked solemnly into her eyes. "No, just one kid."

All the playful happiness drained from Katie's face and she stepped back from him. Away from his grip on her arms. "You're..."

Quickly he shook his head, reaching for her again. "No, I'm not married. I've never been married. But I do have a child."

"A child?"

"Yes. A daughter." He took a deep breath and his hands gripped her arms as if he were afraid she would bolt when he said what he had to say. "A daughter I never knew I had until three months ago."

Katie nodded for him to continue.

"She was adopted almost seven years ago, but I've found her and I want her back."

Katie's eyes were the only things in her face with any color. Everything else had gone a dead white. He didn't have to finish.

She knew, but she could barely get the name out. "Carly."

He affirmed it with a nod.

She turned from him and he let his hands drop, not trying to hold her. She paced once around the living room, her hands to her mouth, then she sank onto the couch.

"It can't be mere coincidence that the daughter you fathered just happens to be the child I adopted. You knew all along, didn't you?"

There was nothing he could do except confess. "Yes."

"You tracked her down, found out her adoptive father was dead, and decided that the easiest way to get your daughter back was to marry her mother." The color was coming back into Katie's face. Lots of it. Cheeks flushed red and eyes sparked cold blue fire.

"No, that's not–"

"I must say, you completely blindsided me on this one." She

stood up, nailed him to the wall with a smoldering glance and held him there while she paced the floor again, never taking her eyes off him. "I've been courted by men who were nice to Carly to try to get me into their beds, men I could have cared for if they had really cared for Carly. I never expected to be sucked in by a man who was nice to me to get to Carly."

"You're wrong. I–"

"Do you deny it?" She stopped in front of him, fists on hips. "Carly is a wonderful child, but I often thought it strange that you seemed to take more of an interest in her than you did in me."

"Maybe at first, but–"

"But then you realized that you could get your child by marrying me? Not too bad of an idea, was it? There were compensations, after all. I'm not that bad looking and you seemed to like my cooking."

"Well, yes, that's all true, but..."

"Was that when you figured that marrying me was a heck of a lot easier way to get your child than resorting to a court battle you'd probably lose?"

She thought he'd lose a court battle? But he wouldn't. His lawyer had assured him of that. If Katie knew he wouldn't lose in court, she'd know he was marrying her for herself. "I won't lose if this goes to court, Katie."

"Is that a threat?"

He shook his head, surprised that she would think he was threatening her. "No, just fact."

"I don't see how you could win. Carly is legally adopted and has been for seven years. She's mine now."

He had to convince her that he wanted her. That he wasn't just proposing so he could get custody of Carly. "I never signed away any rights, Katie."

"Nor have you exercised those rights for seven years. What

makes you think any court would favor you?" She stopped, realization dawning in her eyes. "You've already consulted a lawyer, haven't you?"

"Yes, but—"

"So, what else did he say? What other ammunition can you use against me in a court of law?"

He took a deep breath and decided to lay it all out for her, to let her know just how hopeless her case would be, how sincere he was in wanting to marry her. "I'm one-quarter Commanche. Texas law favors Native Americans in cases like this, especially since I never signed away any rights."

"So, you think I'll just give up and not fight you?"

Adrian's fists went to his hips and he decided to give it to her with both barrels. She had to know he didn't need to marry her to get Carly. "If it comes right down to it, I can afford to keep you in court a lot longer than you can afford to be there."

She suddenly grew very calm. It frightened him more than anything else she could have done. "I want you to leave, Adrian."

Adrian felt like she had just turned a shotgun on him, loaded with scrap iron and shot it full into his belly. What was wrong with her? He wanted to marry her! Didn't she realize that? "Katie, there's no need to—"

"I want you to leave. Now."

She was glaring at him like a mule that would rather die than move one foot, and he knew there was no reasoning with her now. Maybe when she calmed down she'd be a little more reasonable, understand what he wanted. "I'll call you in a few days."

She had her hand on the door, herding him through it. "No, I'll call you."

Adrian heard the door slam behind him. It damn near smacked his butt on his way out and sounded much too final for his peace of mind.

Two days later Katie called.

Adrian had kept his cell phone by his side during those two days afraid he would miss her call.

He had thought it would reassure Katie to know that he really wanted Carly, that he wasn't one of those guys who used Carly to get to her. He had thought it would convince Katie that he really wanted to marry her if she knew he didn't need to marry her to get Carly, that he could get custody of his daughter whether Katie married him or not. That's what he had thought. Unfortunately, that was not what Katie had thought.

For the last two days, each time the phone rang he had grabbed it like a lifeline in a storm. Each time he had been disappointed to hear sales pitches for newspapers, for replacement windows, for siding, for long distance phone companies.

This time, the wild pounding of his heart accelerated when he heard her voice, then came crashing to a near halt at her cold, brusk tone.

"The first thing we need to do is determine whether or not you are actually Carly's father," she said without preamble.

"Katie, I–"

"There's a clinic on San Pedro that does paternity testing. I've already taken Carly. I'd appreciate it if you would go at your earliest convenience."

"At my earliest convenience? Katie, you sound like a damned receptionist. Can I come over?"

"Here's the number. You can call and make an appointment. They'll give you directions." She gave him the name of the clinic and their phone number.

He wrote down the information and repeated it back to her. "Katie, can we talk?"

"They'll send us both a copy of the test results in seven to ten days." She sounded as if she hadn't even heard his question.

"I'll go this afternoon. Katie, at least meet me someplace. Let me—" She hung up.

Adrian stood looking down at the paper in his hand. He had wanted this. He had wanted a genetic test to know for certain that Carly was his. He had thought it was important to know. But now, he suddenly realized that it didn't matter.

Carly was more important to him than any child had a right to be. She was special just because she was Carly, and he wanted to be her father in a real sense, not just the man who had contributed one half of a cell to her being. Sure, it would be nice to know that she really was his. But he didn't think he could love her any more than he already did. If she wasn't his, if he had no right to ever see her again, if Katie refused to marry him, he knew there would forever be a big hole in his heart. No, he corrected himself. Two holes.

He crumpled the paper in his fist. Carly had to be his. It was the only way he would be assured of ever having the right to see her again. Of seeing Katie. Of possibly healing the breach he had caused and becoming a family.

On the other hand, if Carly were not his, it would prove that he wanted to marry Katie for herself. Maybe she would be more ready to accept him when he continued to ask her to marry him even without the ulterior motive of getting custody of his child.

He straightened out the paper. There was only one way to find out for sure. "Oh what tangled webs we weave when first we practice to conceive," he muttered. And with that wry Shakespearean misquote he went to the clinic, then cleared out the apartment and went home to Austin to wait for the results.

Katie had to pry her fingers from the phone, force her teeth to unclench. He wanted to talk. What more was there to say? From now on, he could just let the lawyer he had consulted do his talking.

If she had to listen to Adrian's voice another minute, she'd be begging him to listen to her. It had sounded so good to hear him. Too good. It was like hot molasses and her anger was melting like butter. Two days without him and she was in withdrawal. And he wanted to come over?

She could just imagine trying to stay across the room from him. It would be like a piece of iron and an electromagnet, with every word he said, every gesture he made, turning up the power.

She was angry. She felt like she had been used and manipulated. But she still wanted Adrian.

Katie's hand shook as she let go of the phone and she clasped it in the other one.

She had taken Carly to the clinic that morning, before she called Adrian, so there would be no chance of running into him. Now, she almost wished she had waited. She jerked her hand away from the phone she had absently started caressing as she thought about Adrian. The man was putting her through hell. If he really was Carly's father, it was possible that she could lose her daughter and never see her again. How could she still have feelings for a man who would do that to her?

And not just that, either. He had wormed his way into her heart knowing full well what he was doing, all while keeping her in ignorance.

Looking back on it, she wondered how she could have been so blind. That time in the restaurant when the waitress had commented on how much Carly looked like Adrian, he had nearly choked on his pizza. But he hadn't said anything. Not then, not later. And she had thought it so wonderful that they looked like a real family.

"What did he say?"

Katie started out of her reverie. She had forgotten that Miriam Kisor was there. Angela and Carly were playing in Carly's room.

"He's going to get the test done this afternoon. We should know one way or the other within ten days."

"I still think you should consult an attorney."

"I did."

"I mean an attorney who specializes in adoption law. I'm a corporate lawyer. I don't know much about adoption."

"You suggested the DNA test. I thought that was very good advice. I wouldn't have thought of it."

"Yes, you would have. It's a no-brainer. You were just so stressed out by all this you couldn't think at all. But you need a good lawyer. Someone who knows this area of the law."

Katie stood up again, clenching and unclenching her hands as she paced. "Not if the test comes out negative."

Miriam snorted. "Do you really think it will?"

Katie sat down in the chair next to the couch and dropped her head into her hands. "No."

"Well, then?"

Katie straightened, taking a deep breath. "If it's true, if Adrian really is Carly's father, then maybe I'll call a lawyer."

Miriam stood up, hands on hips and glared down at her friend, "Then, *maybe?*"

Katie stood up again, flinging out her arms, "What if he isn't Carly's father? If he isn't, then all this worry, consulting a lawyer, would just be..."

"Is that what you're hoping? That Adrian isn't her father?"

Katie started to say yes, but stopped. She wasn't sure what she was hoping. If he wasn't, then would he just disappear from her life forever? As angry as she was with Adrian, she wasn't sure she wanted that. But she certainly didn't want to lose her daughter.

"He has asked me to marry him," Katie said weakly.

Miriam took Katie's hands in hers squeezing gently. "And you'd marry him to keep Carly."

"It might be the only way I can keep her." Katie turned and started to pace again. Miriam sat back down on the couch. "I accused him of wanting to marry me to avoid a court battle. If what he said is true, I'll be the one who would want to avoid the court battle."

"There's still a chance–"

"But is it a chance I want to take? You told me the same thing he did, the courts have been favoring natural parents, especially if they didn't give up their rights in the first place—which he didn't—and especially if those parents are Native American—which he is. My only option might be to marry him."

"Is that an option you want?"

"Two days ago it was. Now I don't know." Katie dropped back down next to Miriam. "Two days ago I wanted to marry Adrian more than anything in the world. He obviously cared a lot for Carly and I thought he would make a wonderful father." She gave a quick, wry laugh. "Now I know why."

"He certainly seemed concerned that night she was sick," Miriam said.

Katie remembered how tender Adrian had been with Carly, how attentive, how gently he had carried her home from Miriam's house. She had been so touched by his care. She found herself sitting there mooning over him, a sappy smile on her face. "I never thought I'd find another man I could love as much as I did Brent, who excited me so much. Just thinking about Adrian, I..." Katie felt her nipples pucker and threads of desire beginning to streak up from her groin.

She sobered and clenched her teeth together. "He's also the man who might take Carly away from me."

Chapter Eleven

ADRIAN WORKED AT THE CEDAR FENCE POST. FOR A HALF rotten post it sure was taking a heck of a lot of work to get it out. He'd been riding the fence line since sunup and now it was hot. He took off his Stetson and wiped his face with a blue bandana.

He was on a rocky hill surrounded by cedar, live oak, and cactus. The cactus blooms were almost all gone now, the prickly pear fruit filling out along the edges of the large flat cactus pads. His horse, Sam, stood a few feet away nibbling at a tuft of buffalo grass. As always lately when he took a break, Adrian's gaze swept to the south. It didn't take much of a hill in this country to give a man a view and Adrian could see a long way from this little rise. But not all the way to San Antonio. Not to that little house where his daughter and Katie lived.

The clinic had said it would take about ten days for the test results. But he didn't need test results to know that Carly was his daughter in all the ways that counted. He had to see them. For the past week he had done what he had to, from negotiating new contracts with suppliers to mending fences. He had been away from the business and the ranch too long, but after a week of forgetting the names of long time business associates and nailing his thumb seventeen times a day working on that fence, he knew he had to see them. Even if all he did was drive down their street and see the outside of their house, it would be something. It would be better than this interminable waiting. His mind and heart weren't here. They were in San Antonio.

He clapped his hat back on his head, jury-rigged the fence post to last another few days, and headed back to the ranch house.

He didn't even take the time to change. He handed the reins to a stable hand, jumped in his car, and headed south.

Adrian had never driven that stretch of I-35 faster. It had never seemed to take so long. The twenty minute cutover on Loop 1604 seemed to take a year. But at last he was cruising down their street, looking eagerly ahead to the beige brick mailbox, feeling his heart leap and slamming on the brakes when he saw Katie reaching into the box to take out her mail.

There was only one thing in the mail, a long slim envelope marked with the logo of the clinic. Katie pulled it out and stood staring down at it, afraid to open it, afraid not to. A car skidding to a halt beside her gave her a start and she looked up. She, who never before had paid much attention to cars, could now spot a silver Lexus half a parking lot away. This close there was no doubt who that Lexus belonged to.

The first time she had met him, she had thought Adrian Wright looked dangerous. He looked dangerous now. And exciting. His face was sweat-streaked and set, his blue denim shirt clung damply to his chest and the rolled up sleeves showed off his corded forearms. He had removed his leather work gloves and they dangled from the back pocket of a too snug pair of jeans. He wore no spurs on his Justin Ropers, but it seemed almost as if she could hear the jangle of them anyway as he stalked toward her. She could almost envision a six gun slung at his hip.

It took a real effort not to back away from his approach. But she squared her shoulders, lifted her chin, and looked him in the eye. He stopped within kissing distance, face-to-face and toe-to-toe.

She held up the envelope in the slender space between their bodies. "I take it you got one of these today, too."

Surprised, he looked down at what she held in her hand, puzzled for a moment until she tapped one finger on the return address.

"No. I mean, I don't know. I didn't stop to check the mail."

Then what are you doing here, she wanted to ask. Why have you come if you don't already know what this envelope contains?

"Then I guess you're as anxious to know as I am." She stuck one fingernail under the flap and began to tear the envelope open.

His hand, warm and calloused, closed over hers, stopping her. "It doesn't matter, Katie."

She looked up at him and thought he was going to crash right through all the anger and hurt barricading the way and kiss her right then and there. But she was not ready to be kissed, as much as the idea appealed to her, as much as she remembered the firm feel of his lips on hers.

"What do you mean, 'It doesn't matter'? It mattered enough for you to come looking for your daughter in the first place, didn't it? It mattered enough for you to tangle your life up with ours and threaten to take my child away from me, didn't it?"

"I never threatened to—"

"It mattered enough to bring you back here today."

"But it doesn't matter now."

His hand had tightened on hers, nearly crushing it and she thought he was going to wrench the letter away from her. Why didn't it matter? What was he doing here? Had he found out that he was Carly's father and didn't want to fight her in court? Had he come to renew his marriage proposal? Or had he found out that he wasn't Carly's father and still wanted to marry her? That was a proposal she could accept. One she would know came from desire and not from necessity.

"It matters to me," she said.

He held her hand for another long moment then slowly released it. The envelope was crumpled and she straightened it out, continued tearing it open along the top edge, a jagged, uneven tear that looked more like a wild animal had gotten hold of it than a human. She tugged at the folded paper inside. It caught on one side and she had to stop to finish tearing open the corner before she could pull out the letter.

The sheet of paper was folded in thirds. She lifted the top third. It was only letterhead and date. She opened it the rest of the way and read the brief contents then looked up at Adrian. He had not read over her shoulder. He hadn't had to. He could see the results in her eyes.

"Carly's mine."

Katie shuddered with all his statement implied. He had a right to Carly. Exactly what those rights were might be for a court to decide. But whether he got full custody or just visiting rights, he did have a right to at least a part of Carly. She couldn't imagine a court not giving him something.

Katie bristled. "You might be her natural father, but Carly isn't yours. She's mine."

"And mine," Adrian countered. He was grinning now, as big and as foolishly as any man who has just been told he's a father.

"Mr. Wright!" Carly came slamming out the door and careened down the walk, arms outstretched.

Katie tried to head her off, to stop her before she reached Adrian. But Carly sped past her and jumped into her father's arms, wrapping her legs around his waist and her arms around his neck and squeezing the life out of both. "We've missed you! Where have you been?"

Adrian's face was buried in the curve of Carly's shoulder and he was squeezing her as hard as she was squeezing him. "I've missed you, too, Peanut. I brought you a present."

"You did?"

Adrian leaned back to look at Carly. "It's in the car."

He started toward his car with Carly in his arms and Katie's mouth went dry. He could take Carly with him and there was no way she could stop him. He was bigger and stronger and he was her father. Once he had her in Austin, it would indeed be a court battle with little hope of winning against a rich, powerful family like Adrian's.

Katie started after them, feeling powerless, but determined to keep her daughter. Adrian opened the car door and bent down still with Carly glued to him. It would be so easy for him to just scoot inside, slam the door in Katie's face and take off. Katie managed to snatch hold of Carly's right ankle. She wasn't about to give up her daughter without a struggle, physical and legal.

But Adrian didn't get into the car. He just reached inside and handed a box to Carly, then slammed the door shut.

"Dominos!" Carly said.

Adrian started to turn and that's when he noticed Katie's hold on Carly's ankle, the look of panic in her eyes.

"I told you I'd get you some," Adrian said to Carly, but his gaze never left Katie's. It was an angry, accusing gaze. "I'll teach you to play Chicken Foot," he told Carly.

"Now?"

"No. Not now." He let his daughter slide down to the side-walk, turned her, and smacked her lightly and playfully on the bottom. "Later. Right now I need to talk to your mother. You go on inside."

Carly turned back to give Adrian a final hug around the hips before she ran back in the house calling back, "Thanks, Mr. Wright!"

Adrian looked at Katie a long moment, hurt and sadness in his eyes. "I would never take her like that, Katie. I won't steal Carly away from you."

"No, you won't have to, will you?"

"No, I won't," he agreed, hanging his thumbs in his back pockets. "But I thought you knew me better than to think I would."

"I only know what I'd do," she answered. "And I'd do anything it takes to keep Carly."

"Would you, Katie? Would you marry me?"

"Is that a threat?"

Adrian looked dumbfounded. "A threat? No, it was a proposal." He shrugged. "A mighty poor one, but a proposal."

Katie looked at Adrian. He was handsome and lean and virile. She had never desired a man more than she did this one. She could tell he loved Carly, now more than ever. But did he really love her? Sure, his lawyers had told him he would have no trouble winning custody of Carly in court. But lawyers had been wrong before. Maybe marrying her was his insurance policy.

But what choice did she have? It might take everything she had to fight him in court. He was rich enough to keep her in appeals court for years without noticing a ripple in the family finances. She could end up losing everything and Carly, too.

She had said she would do anything to keep Carly. Marrying Adrian Wright was not such an awful thing. It could have been a wonderful thing if only it was for the right reasons.

"All right, Adrian," she said at last. "I'll marry you." But she couldn't meet his gaze when she said it.

She felt his fingers beneath her chin tilting her head up. He was grinning again. Why shouldn't he be grinning? He was getting everything he wanted, wasn't he? He bent toward her but she flinched away, not wanting to kiss him like this, full of uncertainty and doubt.

He pulled her head back around to face him. "Isn't it traditional to seal a marriage agreement with a kiss?"

She managed a wan smile. "Yes, I suppose it is."

He kissed her then, gently at first, then his arms wrapped around her and he deepened the kiss to near assault. An assault of her senses on all fronts. He tasted of the wild Texas Hill Country and smelled of horse and leather and sweat, and he felt like granite. She couldn't keep her arms from going around him, smoothing over the taut muscles of his back, and he groaned softly in response to her touch.

But it was all bittersweet for Katie. The responses were all the right ones. It was just the reasons that were all wrong.

But the responses were beginning to swamp her senses. She was ready to pull him down on top of her right then if they hadn't been outside. That and a sudden interruption from Carly.

"Mom!"

Katie broke away from Adrian, forcing herself out of her haze. Carly was headed down the walk, the phone in her hand.

"It's Mrs. Grayson. She wants to know about tonight."

Adrian waited while she took the phone.

"Is everything ready for tonight, Katie?" Nelle Grayson's voice was cultured, with the accent of a true Southern belle.

"Yes, Nelle. I already have it all in the car, the rum cake, a carrot cake, two peach pies, four dozen dinner rolls, half with sesame seeds, half with poppy seeds. The rolls are still warm from the oven. I'll be over in just a few minutes."

"You are such a gem, Katie. No one I know bakes like you do. I'll see you in a few minutes, then."

Katie said good-bye and cut the connection, handing the phone back to Carly.

"We need to talk, set a date, make plans," Adrian said.

"I have to go now, Adrian."

"I know. I heard. I could watch Carly for you, be here when you get home."

She shook her head, shoving down the panic she felt, sure that he wouldn't really take the chance to steal Carly, but too afraid to trust him, nevertheless. "She's going to Angela's. I won't be home for a while."

"Tomorrow, then?"

She nodded.

"About noon?"

"Noon's fine. I'll make lunch." She shouldn't have added that last, but Southern hospitality was too deeply inbred in her not to offer someone a meal when they came.

"See you tomorrow, Peanut," Adrian said to Carly as he got into his car. "Maybe we can play a game or two of dominoes. Maybe I can't win at *Chutes and Ladders*, but I'm determined to win at something."

Katie held Carly in front of her, watching Adrian drive away. Adrian had won at something. He was getting Carly after all. He was getting Katie, too, even if it was only a convenience. Her whole life had just changed. She should be feeling joyful. But all she could feel was despair.

Adrian was still grinning when he pulled into the parking lot at the office in Austin. He could hardly wait to tell Jace he had done the right thing and it had all worked out. Carly was really his and Katie was going to marry him.

He couldn't wait to break the news to his parents. They had

been dropping broad hints for years now that it was time for him to find a nice girl, settle down and give them some grandchildren. Wouldn't they be surprised to find out that not only was he getting married, but that Katie's child was their very own blood grandchild.

He hoped he could talk Katie into getting married next week. He wanted them at the ranch now, but he knew it took a few days to arrange things—blood test, license, preacher. But a week should do it.

Of course, women usually liked to make a big fuss over things like this. But Katie had already been married once. Maybe she wouldn't insist on a big dust-up and would settle for just a few family and friends... and soon.

He got out of the car, bounded up the steps of the Wright Oil Company and passed the receptionist with a cheery wave. He sailed blithely past the secretary who was supposed to keep visitors waiting until Jace had a free moment or two, and plunged into his brother's office.

Jace, phone to ear, looked up in surprise then waved his brother to a chair while he finished his call. Adrian looked around for an empty chair and finally moved a stack of files to the floor and sat down, stretching out his long legs and crossing them at the ankles.

"Well! Am I glad to see you!" Jace hung up the phone and stood up to stretch. "Pick a pile and get to work."

Adrian cocked a brow and looked around the room with a jaundiced eye. "Your office looks worse than mine."

"That's because most of this came from your office."

"I thought some of those files looked familiar."

"Yeah, well, we've all taken some of the load for you since you've been in San Antonio. Just like you all took over for me while I was in New Guinea." Jace sat back down, moved a stack of papers out of his way and folded his arms on his desk. "So, how's the San Antonio situation?"

"Katie and I are getting married."

"Congratulations!" Jace jumped up, came around the desk, pumped Adrian's hand and clapped him on the shoulder. "I thought you looked mighty proud of yourself when you came in here."

Jace leaned back against his desk, crossed his arms, and asked soberly, "Did you tell Katie about—"

"I did. We did a genetic check and Carly is definitely mine."

"I guess double congratulations are in order. This calls for a cigar or a beer or something." Jace looked around, then picked up a jar of candy from the desk and held it out to Adrian. "Unfortunately, I don't have anything like that on hand. Would you temporarily settle for a Jolly Rancher?"

Adrian laughed, took one of the candies and stuck it into his shirt pocket. "You owe me one celebration, Brother."

Jace laughed and leaned forward to clap Adrian on the shoulder once more. "You deserve it."

The brothers grinned like fools at each other for several moments before Jace asked, "I guess Katie took the news about you and Carly pretty well."

"Not really." Adrian got up to pace as well as he could between the piles of folders. There was something niggling at the back of his mind. Something that wasn't right.

"Not really?" Jace cocked his head.

Adrian stopped his pacing and turned to face his brother with his hands on his hips. "She was madder'n heck. She threw me out of her house."

"But now she wants to marry you?" Jace was justifiably bewildered.

That was it. That was what was bothering him. "No," he answered thoughtfully, "I don't think she does."

Jace shook his head even more perplexed than ever. "She doesn't want to marry you, but she's going to anyway? Why?"

That was it. That was what was wrong. Adrian looked at Jace and all the joy of Katie's acceptance was gone for him. "She doesn't think she has a choice."

Jace looked at him questioningly.

"Good Lord. I didn't ask Katie to marry me. I gave her an ultimatum."

Chapter Twelve

IT WAS ALMOST NINE O'CLOCK BEFORE KATIE FINISHED AT NELLE Grayson's. She had stayed to help serve and ended up helping to clean up afterward, too. In return, Nelle had given her a hefty bonus and a grateful hug when she left.

When Katie tapped on Miriam Kisor's door she could hear Angela's and Carly's disappointed "Oh no's" before Miriam opened it.

About forty-seven Barbie dolls were scattered over the floor with a complete village of Barbie dream houses, cars, kitchens, and a beauty parlor.

"Sorry to break up your party, girls, but I'm back," Katie said to them.

"Can Angela come home with us and spend the night?" was Carly's immediate response.

Katie laughed. "Sure, if it's all right with her mother."

"It's fine with her mother," Miriam answered. "In fact I was going to ask if you could take Angela for the night. I have a meeting at the office at eight o'clock in the morning about a case that goes to trial on Monday."

Katie bit her lip. "Hmm. Will you be back by noon?"

"I should be. It's just some final details we have to go over. But if there's a problem, Dan can cancel his golf game and stay home with Angela."

Katie looked down at the girls' hopeful faces. "No, no, Angela can spend the night."

Both the girls shouted, "Yeah!" and gave each other conspiratorial grins, as if by their wiles they had somehow tricked their mothers into allowing the overnight.

"Where is Dan?" Katie asked.

"Sleeping. He was exhausted. He was on the construction site at five-thirty every morning this week and he wanted to get some rest before his game tomorrow."

"Do you have a few minutes?"

"Sure. Come on in the kitchen. I think there's still some warm sludge left in the bottom of the coffee pot. If not, I can make a fresh pot."

Katie slid into a chair at the table and accepted the cup of coffee Miriam handed her. "You weren't kidding," she said taking a sip. "This really is sludge."

Miriam wrinkled her nose after tasting her own cup. "Shall I make a fresh pot?"

Katie shook her head, fiddling with the cup handle.

"What's wrong?"

"I've agreed to marry Adrian."

"What!?"

The girls in the living room looked up but went back to their play when nothing life threatening seemed to be taking place in the kitchen.

Miriam leaned forward and lowered her voice, "Are you serious? When did this happen?"

"This afternoon, just before I left." Katie held up a hand to stave off Miriam's why didn't you tell me? "I didn't have time to tell you earlier. But he's coming back tomorrow at noon. We're going to talk about setting a date, make plans." She looked down at the thick white mug with the even thicker black coffee in it.

"That's why you wanted to know if I'd be back by noon, right? Want me to take the girls someplace so you two can be alone?"

Katie nodded. "I'd appreciate it."

"I take it you haven't told Carly yet."

"No. Not yet."

"So, how did this come about?"

"I got the test results today. Carly is his."

"That doesn't mean you have to marry him." Miriam cocked her head, studying Katie. "Unless that's what you want..."

Katie leaned her head into one hand. "I'm not sure what I want anymore. A week ago I was more than ready to marry Adrian. What more could I have asked for? He was completely taken with Carly, he was more physically attractive to me than any man I've ever met, and I thought we were beginning to really care for each other."

"And now all that has changed."

Katie looked up at Miriam, thinking hard. "Has it?"

Miriam's jaw dropped. "The jerk is trying to take your daughter away from you!"

"But he did ask me to come along, too. Maybe nothing has changed at all. He still cares about Carly. I still, God help me, melt inside when I think of him touching me, and he must have some feelings for me. Would he have asked me to marry him if he didn't?"

"If he did have feelings for you, would he blackmail you into marriage by threatening to take your daughter?"

Katie's head fell back into her hands almost dizzy from the same circular argument she had been having with herself since Adrian had proposed.

"I don't know. I just don't know."

Adrian turned down Jace's invitation to go out and celebrate. He had to think. Sam was almost as good a listener as Jace, especially when the horse had a trough full of oats and Adrian was putting a shine to his coat with a curry comb.

Adrian picked at a particularly troublesome tangle in Sam's mane and wondered if he had half the brains the cowpony had. How could he have been so stupid? If Katie wasn't going to be gone this evening, he would have gone right back to San Antonio and groveled at her feet in apology.

"I'd do anything to keep Carly," he kept hearing her say.

And like a dolt, his next words were, "Will you marry me?" What else could she have said but "yes"? And she'd do it, too. Heck, hadn't he thought about marrying Katie to get Carly? It wouldn't have been a bad deal, either. But not if you didn't have a choice. Katie did have a choice but he didn't think she knew that.

She didn't have to marry him to keep her daughter. He wasn't going to take her to court and take Carly away from her. He was sure they could work something out. Two weekends a month wasn't what he wanted. He wanted to pick Carly up after school, take her to ballet classes or piano lessons or whatever it was she wanted to take. He wanted to be around to help with her homework, tuck her in at night, watch *The Little Mermaid* with her curled in his lap.

And he wanted Katie, too. He wanted her in his bed and in his life.

But he'd take Carly two weekends a month if that's all he could have.

The problem was, Katie didn't know that. And if she did, would she still marry him? Heck, she might not even agree to two weekends a month. Then what would he do? Take her to court? Surely it wouldn't come to that. Surely, Katie would be reasonable. She might even marry him even when she knew she didn't have to.

But the uncertainty kept him awake most of the night.

The next morning he refused to let himself leave Austin before ten. Since he couldn't sleep anyway, he went into the office to tackle some of the paperwork that had been piling up. He stared at it, but he kept seeing Katie with that stricken look on her face. How could he have been so immersed in his own happiness that he had failed to notice her misery? He shuffled the papers back and forth for a couple of hours, then put the most urgent stuff in the center of Jace's desk and headed south.

"Mr. Wright!"

Katie heard Carly's joyous yelp and glanced at the clock. Eleven thirty-five. Adrian was early. Too early. Miriam wouldn't be here to pick up the kids for another fifteen or twenty minutes. What was she going to do with Adrian for twenty minutes? Carly would expect everything to be normal, for them to have a good time together, to laugh, to touch, to be glad in each other's company. How could she do that? How could she walk into that living room and act as if there were no issues looming over any possibility of happiness for them?

But she had to do it. For Carly. Just as she would marry Adrian for Carly, and spend the rest of her life with him for Carly.

She heard some scuffling, some laughter-filled shrieks from Carly and Angela, and a couple of "oofs" from Adrian before she heard him ask, "Where's your mom?" and knew she couldn't put off going in there any longer.

"Hello, Adrian."

He looked good standing there with Carly hanging on one leg and Angela slung upside down over his shoulder. Fatherly. The boots and Stetson and jeans were gone. He wore khakis and a sports shirt just like any normal father would to go out on a Saturday morning. His hair was mussed and his shirttail was hanging out on one side from tussling with the girls, and Katie would have liked nothing better than to join in on their romp—if things had been different.

But Carly didn't know that. She ran to Katie and tugged on her hand, pulling her toward Adrian. "Come on, Mom!" And Katie went. For Carly's sake, of course. Just for Carly's sake.

Adrian held a squirming Angela with one arm and put the other around Katie, and she allowed it, for Carly's sake. And it felt so good. Too good. He smelled of soap and aftershave this morning instead of horse and leather, and she wasn't sure which she preferred. Both were Adrian and both were exciting. She should push him away. Keep him at arm's length. No, farther. But she couldn't. And she wouldn't fool herself. It wasn't just because of Carly. And it was in spite of everything that should be keeping her away from him.

She smiled for Carly's sake, though, and knew she would go through with this marriage for Carly's sake. She smiled and straightened away from Adrian, stepping back. It had been all too easy to find herself beginning to love Adrian. She would have to guard well what was left of her heart. She didn't want to give it wholly to a man who would blackmail a woman into marriage, to a man she wasn't sure loved her at all.

"I was just starting lunch," she said, retreating toward the kitchen, glad she had managed to keep the tremor out of her voice.

"I know I'm early, but I..." Angela managed to kick free and Adrian lowered her to the floor rather than let her fall. But he got in a last tickle before she escaped with Carly to whisper together and plan their next attack.

He looked up at Katie, now halfway back to the kitchen and he seemed just as much at a loss for something to say as she was.

He had to be wondering if they were going to have any time alone. Then both girls hit him at once from opposite sides, trying to drag him down. They were no match for him, but he fell to the floor anyway with both of them on top of him trying to pin him down.

"I give, I give!"

The girls cheered, and plopped onto the floor beside him, cheeks pink, hair mussed, breath coming fast. Adrian half sat up, propped on his elbows.

"Miriam will be here soon. She's going to take the girls to a movie."

Adrian yanked one of Carly's loosened braids. "Then I'm glad I came early so I didn't miss seeing them."

"Can we play dominoes now, Mr. Wright?"

"Sure. Go get them."

The girls ran to Carly's room to get the dominoes and Adrian sat up, running a hand through his hair to straighten it, then sitting with knees bent and his arms around them, hands linked. "I'm glad Carly is still here, but I'm glad we'll have a chance to talk, Katie. Your friend, Miriam, is a real treasure."

She nodded, fiddling with the kitchen towel she still held in her hands. He might not think so well of Miriam if he knew she wanted Katie to hire a lawyer to deal with this situation. "She's been a good friend." She could just as easily have said, *She's on my side. Whatever happens, Miriam will be pulling for me.*

"I guess it hasn't been easy being a single parent, has it?"

Katie shrugged. No, it wasn't easy. All the worry was hers all of the time. And you had to depend on friends if you needed time alone or an evening out. She loved Carly with all of a natural mother's passion, but sometimes, just sometimes, it would be nice to have another adult to share with, to talk to, to have someone to watch TV with without having to watch *Sesame Street* or a Disney film, to have someone share the driving, someone else to sign a permission slip from school or go to a PTA meeting. "I miss Brent," she said. It was not the most tactful thing to have said in the circumstances. But she did miss Brent. She always would.

Adrian's mouth tightened. She could see his jaw clench. "I guess you would."

She was glad he didn't suggest that she wouldn't have to miss Brent any longer now that she was marrying him. On the other hand, she was almost angry at his understanding. And maybe she was just trying to find fault, to build her defenses against caring for him any more than she already did.

"Here they are!" Carly and Angela sat down on the floor, forming a triangle with Adrian, and dumping the dominoes out between them. "What do we do first?"

Katie left them to play and went into the kitchen to finish the lunch, glad to escape, dreading the time when she and Adrian would be alone, planning a wedding neither of them wanted. Maybe it would all work out. Maybe a modern marriage of convenience could work out just as well as they did in all those Regency romances she'd read.

Miriam was going to take the girls out for pizza so Katie just had to make something for herself and Adrian. She cut up carrots and celery and onion and dropped them into the chicken broth she had simmering along with some chopped up cooked chicken. She had made noodles a couple of days ago which she would add during the last few minutes.

She pulled out a loaf of rye bread she had made just the day before and sliced some for sandwiches. She had pie dough in the freezer and apples in the fridge, but she had refused to let herself go to the trouble of making a pie even though she knew it was Adrian's favorite. Because it was Adrian's favorite. He could just make do with one of the peanut butter cookies she and Carly had made yesterday afternoon. It was all ready by the time the doorbell rang and she heard Carly let Miriam in.

Katie hurriedly wiped her hands. Miriam was a good friend. A loyal friend. A friend who would stand by her through anything. Miriam also had no hesitation about ripping to shreds anyone who hurt, or even threatened to hurt, one of her own. Hopefully, Miriam would restrain herself knowing that Katie might end up marrying Adrian. Hopefully, she wouldn't feel the need to get in a few licks before he even knew she was his opponent. In any case, Katie thought she had better get out there before Adrian found himself in a verbal duel that could only leave him bloodied and dying on her living room floor.

Miriam had already sent the girls to get their things and straighten their hair and she stood there glaring at Adrian with a look on her face that would have made even Torquemada's blood run cold.

Adrian had risen and was tucking in his shirttail, one dark brow cocked, his mouth a tight line as he eyed Miriam. It looked as if they were squaring off for battle and Katie, not wanting either of them to say something they would regret later, forced a cheery smile and stepped between the opponents.

"Miriam, thank you so much for taking the girls. Did you get all the details of that case taken care of?"

Miriam knew a distracting ploy when she saw one, but, loyal to her friend, let herself be distracted.

Miriam may have been willing not to slice Adrian to ribbons for Katie's sake, but she leaned closer to Katie as if taking a stand by her friend, and smiled overly sweetly at Adrian as she spoke, as if her words were meant for him, a challenge tossed down. "All taken care of. I don't think we'll have any problem winning our case in court."

Adrian glanced from one woman to the other, and with a tilt of his head, took up the challenge. "I imagine it's best if things can be settled out of court."

"True," Miriam answered. "But sometimes one side wants more than they can have."

Adrian looked at Katie. "And sometimes there are misunderstandings as to what each side wants. Or is willing to settle for."

Katie's breath caught. She looked into his eyes, dark, intent, holding her. "And why would the side with the better chance of winning make concessions?" Katie asked.

Adrian stepped closer to her. She could smell the light, fresh scent of his cologne, feel the heat from his body. "Because sometimes that's the only way to get what they really and truly want."

Carly? Wasn't Carly what he really and truly wanted? Wasn't his daughter what he had come looking for in the first place? Was marrying Katie the concession he was willing to make to insure that he got his daughter? What kind of marriage would they have based only on that?

But was there really any other choice for her? It was entirely possible that she could lose Carly completely. That Adrian could gain sole custody. In that case would she ever see her daughter again?

And what about Carly? Even if Adrian was willing to share custody, Carly could end up shuffled back and forth between them, never sure where she really belonged, being bribed with all the wealth Adrian had at his disposal, spoiled, then sent home to be faced with a mother who not only could not afford ponies, but who insisted on good behavior. It was not the best way to grow up. Katie knew that first hand. It was not what she wanted for her daughter. Her daughter. Hers.

"We're ready!" Carly and Angela burst into the room, hair smoothed, Barbie dolls in hand, faces beaming.

Katie's gaze remained locked with Adrian's. It was only when Carly stepped between them, reaching up to give them both a hug, that Katie broke the gaze. Carly held an arm out to each of them and in unison she and Adrian bent to have their necks squeezed, their shoulders touching, their arms entwining across Carly's back. Katie could feel the fierce possessiveness of Adrian's hug and knew he would never give Carly up. Never.

"Let's go," said Miriam, opening the door. The girls bounced outside and Miriam reached over to give Katie a quick encouraging hug before she followed the girls out.

Chapter Thirteen

KATIE CLOSED THE DOOR, STILL ABLE TO HEAR THE GIRLS deciding to sit together in the back seat so they could play with their Barbie dolls together. She didn't have to turn around to feel Adrian's presence, to know that he still stood as close to her as they had been when Carly drew them together for her parting hug.

She could still feel the heat from his body. Her hand could still feel the bulge of his forearm as it had hugged Carly. They had hugged Carly together and sent her out with her friend just like any married couple would have done. Just like they would probably do many times in the future. Held together in a marriage neither of them wanted by the hug of a child neither could give up.

No, that wasn't quite right. She wanted this marriage. Had wanted it, when she thought Adrian wanted her for herself. And still wanted it, God help her. Still wanted it. She wanted Adrian, she wanted the life she had envisioned, and she wanted his touch.

Physically, she was pretty sure the desire was mutual. But that alone, or even that combined with Carly, was not enough. But it would have to be, wouldn't it?

She turned then to Adrian, unable to keep the pain out of her eyes. He reached for her and she wanted more than anything to

lean into his embrace, to let him convince her that there was more
to his proposal than a convenient way to get his daughter. To feel
his strong arms around her, the stirrings of a desire she had not felt
since...

But there was a wedding to be planned, a date to set, a guest
list to be made. A hundred details to settle. She straightened, plas-
tered a smile on her face that she hoped didn't look as fake as it
felt, and said, "Lunch is ready. I'm sure you must be as hungry as
I am."

He looked as if he wanted to say something, but then he
stepped back, allowing her to lead the way.

The plate of sandwiches was already on the table, covered by
a piece of plastic wrap. He removed it while she filled their soup
bowls and poured a glass of water for each of them.

They ate their meal in near silence, broken only by tight, constrained, pleasantries. "Would you like some more?" and "This is
delicious."

Katie managed half a sandwich and some of her soup in spite
of the knot filling most of her stomach. She noticed that Adrian's
appetite was not quite as hearty as usual, either.

When they were done, Adrian stood to help her clear the
table. She started to object, but he said, "I've been here before,"
reminding her of her saying that the first time you come, you are
company, and after that you are family. They shared a child. They
were going to be planning their wedding this afternoon. He was
certainly family now. She could have no objection to his helping
with the dishes.

In silence, they washed and put away the dishes. A silence
that could have been quite companionable if there had not been so
many questions lying unanswered between them.

Adrian started the coffee while she put away the last of the
dishes and got out two mugs, remembering he liked the Cincinnati

Reds one. She arranged some of the peanut butter cookies on a plate and set it on the table, the sound of glass on wood jarring in the constrained silence.

He poured coffee into the mugs, the sound as noticeably loud and enticing as a television coffee commercial.

She sat at the table, pushed her coffee aside and brought out a legal pad. Forcing a smile to her lips, she took pen in hand, looked directly at Adrian and tried to be as bright and brisk sounding as she could. "I guess the first thing we need to do is decide on a date." He opened his mouth to speak, but she hurried on. "I was thinking next June. Right after school is out."

She had thought a lot about the date. She was not anxious to rush into a loveless marriage. If she could delay things as much as possible, things could go on the way they were for a long time, as far as she was concerned. She would have Carly, but not have a husband who did not love her. She would not have to share custody. It would not last forever, but it would last for a while. Yes, a long engagement was just what she had decided on. A very long engagement.

"Next June?" Adrian came halfway out of his chair spluttering coffee.

Katie smiled saccharine sweetly at him. "Do you have a problem with that?"

"I was thinking about next week."

She raised her brows innocently. "Oh? Are you that anxious to get Carly?"

Adrian placed his palms on the table and leaned over it, looking as menacing as a feral wolf. She had to force herself not to flinch. When he spoke, he sounded like a wolf growling. "I'm that anxious to get you."

Katie's brows arched in surprise. She had not expected that reaction. She had expected annoyance, but compliance. She hadn't expected this.

Before she could reply or even think what to say, he was coming around the table, faster than any wolf after prey. Yanking the pen out of her hand, he tossed it over his shoulder and lifted her out of the chair by her shoulders until she stood facing him, held captive not only by his grip, but the fierceness of his expression.

"Katie Simmons, I want you. I love you. I want you to marry me. But I'm not going to force you to marry me. I want you for my wife and I want you in my bed. But this has to be mutual or it will never work. I want you but I'm not going to use Carly to get you. And I'm not going to use you to get Carly. I won't take her away from you."

He paused and took a long slow breath. "So, Katie, will you marry me?"

Katie felt like a shock wave had hit her and she didn't know what to say. He was giving her everything she wanted. Everything. He had told her he loved her, that he wasn't going to force her, that, most of all, he wouldn't take Carly. But could she trust that? Did he really love her? What if Carly was out of the picture? Would he still want her then?

She stood there a long time considering the possibilities before she asked him, "What if I say no?"

His shoulders slumped and he looked like he had been kicked in the gut by an angry mule. "I don't know. I certainly wouldn't be happy about it."

He let go of her and ran a hand through his hair. "Hell, Katie, I'd be more than unhappy. I'd be devastated. Don't say no."

She looked down, uncertain. She had to know what he would do about Carly if she didn't marry him. He had said he wouldn't take Carly away from her, but what would he expect? She was not going to allow her to be shuffled back and forth between them. She'd lock herself into a loveless marriage first. Not that this would be a loveless union if he meant what he said.

"I mean, what would happen if I say no?"

"Happen?" He looked puzzled for a moment. Then he stepped close to her again, and, grinning, lifted her chin. "I guess I'd keep coming around trying everything I knew to persuade you to change your mind."

She shook her head, freeing herself from his mind-numbing touch, stepping back and putting her chair between them. "No, I mean what would happen to Carly?"

"Carly?" He sounded like he had never heard of her before. He scratched his head and thought a moment. "I guess we could work out something. I'd want to see her as much as I could. I've missed her first seven years. I don't want to miss any more of the rest of her life than I have to. And of course I'd provide for her."

"Provide for her? What do you mean by that?"

He shrugged. "I know you've been a stay-at-home mother and I really admire your parenting. But it can't have been easy not having much of an income."

Katie's fists went automatically to her hips. "Does Carly look deprived?"

"No, no, not at all." He backed up a step, waving his hands between them.

Katie advanced on him, jaw thrust forward, the she-wolf defending her child. "Is this what all this talk of marriage is really about? You've not been a part of her life for seven years but now you can just waltz in here and throw some money around and everything will be okay?"

Adrian did some advancing of his own then, matching her fists on hips stance. "Do you think I wouldn't have been part of her life right from the beginning if I had known about her? Hell, no, money doesn't make up for those lost years. I don't know if anything can. I just don't want to lose any more time. As for providing for her, I know you've been baking to make some extra money. Carly was so happy that one day that she was going to get a new dress because you had a job. I assumed a little extra cash wouldn't hurt your situation."

"You assumed wrong, then. We're doing just fine, thank you. Brent was nuts on insurance and left us very well provided for. I bake because I want to bake. I've stayed at home with Carly because I wanted to stay at home with her. But she's in school now and I need something to do with my time. I've always wanted my own business so I'm starting one. If I tell Carly I'll buy her a dress because I have a job it's because it's a real thrill to me to give her something with money I've earned myself. We are not living from hand-to-mouth and we don't need a rich father coming in here claiming all Carly's affection because he can give her a pony!"

She tried not to let the tears well up in her eyes. She didn't want to cry. But she always cried when she was angry. It made her look weak and she hated it, but she couldn't help it. She managed to dash most of the tears away with the back of her hand and look Adrian in the eye. He looked stunned.

"Do you think that's what I'm doing? Trying to steal Carly's affection from you?"

She turned away to grab a napkin off the table and wiped her eyes before she answered him. "Maybe not trying, but it would happen. Weekends on a ranch with a pony then back to Mom and school and homework?" A few more tears were leaking out. She tried to sniff them up.

Adrian took her face in his hands wiping away the tears with his thumbs. "Back home to Mom? Won't you be at the ranch with us? How will I court you if I'm in Austin with Carly and you're here with What's-His-Name next door?"

"Mitch?" She couldn't help but laugh through the tears at that one.

"Yeah, Mitch."

All she could do in answer was roll her eyes. Adrian got the message.

His hands slid to her shoulders. "Carly means a lot to me. She's my kid. She'd mean a lot to me even if she weren't mine. I love kids. I wanted to have half a dozen. But you're more important to me than more kids." He shrugged. "You adopted Carly. We can adopt some together. They don't have to be my own."

"What are you talking about? Why would we adopt more kids?"

"Didn't you say you wanted a lot of kids, too?"

"Yes, but why couldn't we have our own?"

"Because you can't have kids."

"Whatever made you think that?" Katie's eyes rounded with sudden understanding. "You thought I couldn't have kids because Brent and I adopted Carly?"

Adrian shrugged. "Yeah. Didn't you tell me that?"

Katie laughed. Adrian really did love her. Her. He wanted kids and wanted to marry her even thinking she couldn't have any.

"Adrian, there's no reason I can't have kids. I'm fine. It was Brent who couldn't have children."

"Brent?" Adrian looked like he had been struck dumb.

"It isn't always the woman's fault, you know, you big male chauvinist."

"You mean...?"

She nodded. "There's no reason we can't have that houseful of kids we both wanted."

He laughed and scooped her up, swinging her around. "You mean I get Carly and you and more kids?" He set her down abruptly. "That is what you mean, isn't it? You're saying yes? You'll marry me?"

"I'm saying yes. Yes, yes, and yes."

About the Author

When she spent a year's sabbatical in San Antonio with her husband Ron and their two daughters, Kira and Shana, Michele never knew it would inspire a contemporary romance. After all, she lives in a 165-year old log cabin, weaves. spins, and makes her own soap. But when the plot for *Mr. Right's Baby* popped into her head, she just knew she had to write the story.

Michele also has several historical romances published by Mythical Press, including *Fortune's Foe* and *Conquest of the Heart,* all available from major online retailers.

You can contact Michele at Stegman14@yahoo.com or through her web site at www.michelestegman.com.

www.ingramcontent.com/pod-product-compliance
Lightning Source LLC
Chambersburg PA
CBHW030613130626
46552CB00002B/542